Dutch thought of where he was and where he wanted to be.

He contemplated his next move, knowing that stealing cars was a thing of the past. He would always love the thrill of the chase, of stealing cars, of speeding. But the short bid he had served brought on an accelerated maturity, and he realized that the rewards were no longer worth the risks. He wanted bigger rewards. His mother's unusual and unexpected talk had convinced him of what he had already known.

He could never go back to prison.

He thought about an offer Angel had made to get Barrett to put him on. Dutch couldn't see it though, nickel and dimin' for somebody else. Hell no! That wasn't for Dutch, but the lines had been drawn while he was away.

He was young, black, and free, with nothing to lose, and there was nothing more dangerous than that combination.

Just then an idea hit him like a brick in the face, so hard it almost physically staggered him. *Kill Kazami! Take Kazami and his blocks.*

"A major pioneer of street fiction."
—*Library Journal*

*Please turn this page
for praise for Teri Woods . . .*

RAVES FOR THE *TRUE TO THE GAME* TRILOGY

"Raw . . . gutsy."
—*Essence* on *True to the Game II*

"Four out of five . . . Wonderful . . . a great story . . . a fast-paced exciting read that will surely keep you on your toes."
—Urban-Reviews.com on *True to the Game II*

"Explosive . . . excellent . . . masterful . . . A must-have . . . definitely worth waiting for . . . solidifies Ms. Woods's place as one of the Queens of Street Lit."
—The RAWSISTAZ Reviewers on *True to the Game II*

"Vividly depicts the 1990s drug culture . . . urban fiction fans will welcome the melodramatic final entry in bestseller Woods's True to the Game trilogy."
—*Publishers Weekly* on *True to the Game III*

DUTCH

THE FIRST OF A TRILOGY

Special Collector's Edition

TERI WOODS

GRAND CENTRAL
PUBLISHING

NEW YORK   BOSTON

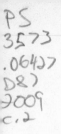
PS
3573
.06437
D8)
2009
c.2

This book is a work of fiction. Names, characters, places, and incidents are the product of the author's imagination or are used fictitiously. Any resemblance to actual events, locales, or persons, living or dead, is coincidental.

Previously published by Teri Woods Publishing, 800 River Road, Suite #3, Edgewater, NJ 07020

Grand Central Publishing
Hachette Book Group
237 Park Avenue
New York, NY 10017

Visit our website at www.HachetteBookGroup.com.

Printed in the United States of America

First Grand Central Publishing Edition: September 2009
10 9 8 7 6 5 4 3 2 1

Grand Central Publishing is a division of Hachette Book Group, Inc.
The Grand Central Publishing name and logo is a trademark of Hachette Book Group, Inc.

Library of Congress Control Number: 2009922679
ISBN: 978-0-446-55153-3

Book design by Giorgetta Bell McRee

This book is dedicated to Chucky Booker, my big brother. For everything you do for my boys, Lucas and Brandon, you are the best uncle in the world. And for babysitting me in my darkest hours, I do love you.

And to my assistant, Tracey Braithwaite, I truly thank you for all your dedication and hard work. Your loyalty is priceless; it's like a commercial.

ACKNOWLEDGMENTS

I would like to thank my family, Phyllis and Corel, Chucky, Dexter and Judy, Andrew, Christopher, Carl, my children, Jessica, Lucas, and Brandon.

DUTCH

CHAPTER ONE

◆

OPENING STATEMENTS

Is the state ready to proceed with its opening statement?"

"Yes, Your Honor, we are," said District Attorney Anthony Jacobs as he turned to look at the defendant, Bernard James, aka Dutch.

He couldn't help but sneer as his lips tightened, eyeing the notorious Dutch. He savored the sight of the Armani-clad black man as he imagined the wooden chair Dutch would sit in while begging for his life as electric shocks jolted the breath out of him. Jacobs had been waiting for this moment his whole life. The day he'd prosecute and convict the infamous "Dutch." Anthony Jacobs had risen through the District Attorney's Office by making himself indispensable to his mentor, District Attorney Fred Ligotta. Old Man Ligotta, as Jacobs referred to him, had brought Anthony up, priming him for this very moment.

Ligotta himself had an illustrious career. He managed to amass the most trial convictions of all of his New Jersey contemporaries within the last thirty years. And although most DAs preferred a plea to a long and costly trial, Ligotta never gave a defendant the option. *It's not my fuckin' money. Besides, any time some piece of shit breaks the law in my county, I want the bastard to pay in full.* And they usually did, either under the table into Ligotta's pockets or by serving years in prison. It was Ligotta's way of saying either pay through the nose or pay out the ass. But, then there was Dutch, the only trophy that had constantly eluded Ligotta, and he was now sitting across the floor at Jacobs's mercy.

How the fuck does a piece of shit nigger like Dutch keep getting away? Christ! This was Ligotta's attitude whenever an informant conveniently came up missing or the police seemed to make stupid errors that allowed cases to be dismissed. *Why don't they make those errors with anyone else?* Ligotta was constantly questioning the cat with nine lives. Even judges seemed to shy away from cases dealing with him. Dutch's talons were sunk deep in the machinery of the city and Ligotta died not knowing why or how. But, for some strange reason, within the past few years, lady luck had defected from Dutch's camp as top men in Dutch's organization took big falls, landing right in Jacobs's lap. *I know you're smiling, old man,* Jacobs told himself as he thought of Old Man Ligotta. *I got him.* And this was true. Jacobs did have Dutch where he wanted him. Along with the informants, there was a mountain of evidence, and even though it was all circumstantial, it was enough for Jacobs to do what Ligotta had failed to. And it felt good, damn good. Nothing, not graduating law school, not his first conviction, not even his election as district attorney, could compare to the feeling of power and surge of potency he felt as his dick hardened right there in the courtroom, something that rarely happened outside the courthouse, let alone in it. As he rose, he tried to discreetly readjust his crotch, then cleared his throat and approached the jurors' box.

"Ladies and gentlemen of the jury, I am District Attorney Anthony Jacobs and I want to thank you for your attendance. I know some of you may deem my gratitude unwarranted, because I am sure if you didn't have to be here, you wouldn't."

The jurors acknowledged the truthfulness of his statement with slight body gestures and nervous smiles.

"But who would be here? I know I wouldn't. Trust me, I feel the same as you. I do. I mean, I would love to be somewhere playing golf or at my daughter's piano recital or just enjoying a quiet day at home, but I can't. I can't because this is my duty," he said as he brought his hand down firmly on the jurors' box railing to emphasize his point. "It is my duty to be here just like it is yours. Your duty to assure your fellow citizens, whom you represent, who are playing golf, or at the piano recital or just relaxing at home, that the streets will remain safe to do such things. Just as it is the duty of the police to do the same for you and me," then, pausing, he added, "duty," for more effect. "But above and beyond our civic duty, above and beyond the inconvenience, duty sometimes imposes on the dutiful; therefore, it is our right!"

The word "right" got the attention of the apathetic yet patriotic all-white jury, as it would that of any other red-blooded American of their ilk.

"It is your right to be safe in your homes. It is your right to oversee justice and the workings of your judicial system and it is your right to be heard as citizens. Especially when citizenship is taken for granted and . . ." he paused, glancing over at Dutch.

Who the fuck he think he looking at? thought Dutch to himself as he eyeballed Jacobs's cracker ass right back.

". . . when the uncivilized play mockery on our sense of security," said Jacobs, finishing his sentence.

Who the fuck he think he calling uncivilized? Dutch thought of the nerve this guy had as he listened.

Jacobs walked slowly away from the jurors' box as he cleaned his glasses. Turning back to them, he placed his glasses on his face and began again in a more subtle tone.

"I know we are all God-fearing human beings, and those here who aren't, well, you wouldn't be here if you didn't recognize the law, and you certainly wouldn't be sitting here if you didn't know the difference between right and wrong. So, I say to you, what if I could present to you the very embodiment of wrong?" he questioned, pointing straight at Dutch. "What if the cause of murder, thievery, victimization, and cruelty stood before you? Would you hesitate to look wrong in the face? Would you banish wrong from our society? Would you turn away from guilt if it were staring you in the face?"

No one budged. The jurors were too busy remembering all the wrong that had ever been done to them and feeling Jacobs's every word as if he was preaching to them from a Bible. Dutch just looked at the jurors as they sat there listening to this motherfucker like he was Santa Claus or somebody. One lady was taking notes, another had her mouth open, and an old man was clinging to Jacobs's every word. *You got to be kiddin' me.*

Jacobs stood there, inwardly smiling gleefully, as the look of vindication subtly played across the faces of the jurors. *I knew I'd get them with my opening statement.* Jacobs had picked the jurors sitting before him precisely and to the T. Despite Dutch's defense team's attempts to dilute the jury pool, Jacobs had succeeded with this jury.

"Ladies and gentlemen of the jury, I know what you would do if given that chance. I'm here today to give it to you. I will prove to you beyond any reasonable doubt that Bernard James, aka Dutch, is the embodiment of this city's wrong. He is the root cause of the blanket of fear prevalent in this city and the degradation of our civil order. It all stems from the actions of this man!" blustered Jacobs as he pointed his finger straight at Dutch's head.

"Yo, man, who he think he pointin' at like that and shit?" whispered Dutch as he leaned into the ear of Michael Glass, lead counsel for his defense team.

"Don't pay him any mind; just act like you're writing notes. Don't let the jury see you get upset," said Michael Glass as he watched Jacobs give his opening statement.

"I will show a path of corruption and waywardness for this man's short life of twenty-eight years. Bernard James is an instigator, an antagonist, and he's the head of the organized crime that has terrorized New Jersey for the past twelve years."

Jacobs stopped for a moment and wiped the sweat from his brow with his silken handkerchief as he gauged the temperament of his captive audience. He felt satisfied, so he continued in the same vein to drive it on home.

"Ladies and gentlemen of the jury, I will prove to you that no man, no woman, and no child will be safe in this city until this man, Bernard James, is behind bars for the rest of his life. So, I'm giving you the chance of a lifetime today to do what no man under the sun has ever had a chance to do . . . find guilt in Bernard James and destroy him. I'm giving you the chance to look evil and wrong in the face and once and for all in the name of the state of New Jersey say that one word: guilty. Ladies and gentlemen, it may be your duty to oversee justice, but it's your right to guarantee your own safety. Thank you."

District Attorney Anthony Jacobs looked over at Dutch as he slowly returned to his seat and sat down. The only thing missing for the starry-eyed jurors was the closing of a curtain.

CHAPTER TWO

♦

IVY HILL

Delores Murphy picked up the morning edition of the *Star Ledger* once again to read the headlines splashed across it like the still-fresh blood of a dying victim. *Trial of the Century Begins Today,* she read to herself. Underneath was a picture of her son, Bernard James, being led into the courtroom with his lawyers in tow. She let the paper fall from her limp hand and hugged herself as if the room had suddenly turned cold. She shivered as she approached the double-glass doors that led to her balcony overlooking the city. As she looked down from her thirtieth-floor penthouse apartment, it seemed to her that the earth and its inhabitants were tiny. But, when she looked up, the heavens seemed vast.

"Please, Lord, I know who he is and I know what he done become, but he mines, Lord. He all I got," she said, frowning as if God was supposed to know that. It was the umpteenth time she had prayed since awakening three hours ago.

She glanced at the antique clock to see that it was only nine-thirty in the morning. She knew the trial was set to begin at 9:00 A.M., and she wondered what would be the fate of her only child, her only son. She delicately reached for the bone china teacup, half filled with herbal tea, and took a sip. The warm steam from the tea soothed her confused mind, but only momentarily. She was so torn between the blood of her son and the blood she knew her son had spilled. It was an evil, twisted plot she knew she was a character in, and knowing what her son deserved in this lifetime and in the next was an ache only a mother could feel when wanting to protect all she had.

She looked around the million-dollar penthouse Dutch had bought her on the East Side of Manhattan and she thought of her beach house in Boca Raton, Florida, and her place in the Hamptons overlooking the bay.

"Son, what's an old lady like me need so many homes for?" she had asked him one day.

"Wherever it rains, I want you to have a roof over your head."

Then he copped the joint in Southern California for close to a mil, even though it never rains there.

Just then as she thought of her son's insatiable smile, the phone rang. She didn't even look at the caller ID box. She just sat in silence thinking of the many gifts Dutch had lavished upon her over the years, changing her destiny, changing her life, and changing her fate as he had changed his own. She heard her machine off in the distance, "I'm not home right now . . ." and then the beep sang in as a familiar voice came through the speaker.

"Yo, Ma, it's me, Chris. Dutch . . . I mean, Bernard told me to call and check up on you. I guess you sleep, but when you get my message call me and let me know you all right."

She heard Chris's voice and a smile stretched across her

face and she felt the warmth of the sun as it beamed down on her. Chris, aka Craze, was her son's best friend, or rather his only friend, and the only person besides Dutch who knew the numbers to reach her.

He called my baby that stupid name, Delores thought to herself, hating the word "Dutch," clinging forevermore to Bernard James, Jr., her only love's son. But to the world, he was Dutch, the most feared black gangster to hit New Jersey in thirty years. Her mind traveled back over the years to the beginning, to the love that had started it all.

The year was 1971 and Newark was in a state of slow recovery from the devastating effects of the riots four years earlier. It had all been over regentrification of the Central Ward and the plan to convert too much of the area to an overly expensive hospital. But that wasn't all. The truth was there was overtly practiced racism within the city's political system and total corruption of the police force during the 1960s. All of this, coupled with the militancy of the young impoverished blacks, added up to one thing. TOO MUCH! The answer from the city was a resounding, NO MORE! So, once a black cabdriver was pulled over in 1967 in an infamous traffic stop and was shot, Newark brothers were up in arms. Things would never be the same, and nevertheless, nothing changed. A black mayor was elected in an effort to stop crime, but the riot continued to fester, leaving whole areas devastated and whole city blocks looking like an old woman with a toothless smile.

Delores was seventeen at the time of the riots. Her mother had raised her in a strict Christian environment, or as strict as poverty would allow the hungry to be. 'Cause when there's nothing to eat on the table, nobody blames you for eating from under the table, not even the Lord. So, Delores's mother did the best she could under the circumstances and Delores had respect, if not love, for her mother. But after the lawlessness of the riots and the exhilaration the disenfranchised feel whenever given a chance to attack the enfranchised, Delores's mother lost her to the riots . . . literally.

Delores was over her girlfriend's house in the projects the day the riots broke out. From the eleventh-floor window she could see the tanks of the National Guard rumble down the middle of the streets surrounded by soldiers carrying automatic weapons. She saw the distant fires and smelled the smoke of the near-raging flames.

"I don't give a damn. They need to burn all this shit down. Who the fuck built this muhfucker and a black man can't even live like a man in this fuckin' country. It's 1967, man. When this shit gonna stop? When they gonna stop fucking with us? They fuck over us, keep a muhfucker making a fuckin' law to lock a nigga up and don't nobody say shit. It's 1967! Now that we say we not gonna take it, and try to stand up for some shit, these crackers got the National Guard coming through this bitch!" screamed Horace, some friend who was drinking C&C out in the living room with Delores's girlfriend's mother.

"Man, we need to go down there and fight!" said another dude.

"Man, if I go down there, I'm killing them muhfuckers, you hear me? And it's gonna be some Huey Newton shit over this bitch, god damn. Yeah, it's gonna be war, if I go down that muhfucker!" said Horace, sippin' some more of that C&C, knowing what might have to be done if he had to get out that chair.

The gunfire rumbled Newark, New Jersey, and thundered through the air and Delores felt so liberated at that moment, so proud to be black. You damn right, all this fuss, all this attention, all this power to fight, all because they killed that black man. *Mmm hmm, y'all gonna see about fuckin' with us,* Delores felt like shouting from the rooftops.

"Look! There go Ms. Bennett! Damn, she got a nice TV," shouted Delores as she signaled for her girlfriend, Arnette, to take a look.

"Where'd she get that from?" asked Arnette, a little slow.

"Girl, where you think? She stole it!" Delores exclaimed as if she was a seasoned riot veteran. "We need to get us one," added Delores.

"Girl, is you crazy? They killin' black people out there! You know Sharon? Her brother got shot on Springfield Avenue last night and he wasn't doin' nothing. Her mama said he was just standing on the corner waiting for the bus. I ain't goin' out there," said Arnette, shaking her head. "Why don't you go out there?" she asked Delores right back, leaning away and folding her arms across her breasts as screams of sirens filled the room and an ambulance sped down the block. "Ain't no telling who's in there," said Arnette warning Delores of what evils lurked outside.

Delores wanted to know firsthand what was goin' on even though she feared what was on the other side of the door. She turned on her heel and grabbed her coat on her way out the bedroom door.

"Where you going?" asked Arnette nervously.

The slamming door answered her question. Delores was

out the house in a flash. However, the moment she set foot
on the cold street concrete, she knew she had made a mistake. For one moment, she turned around, ready to dash
back into the safety of Arnette's apartment, but deep inside
something stopped her and she felt calm and her fears di-
minished. She headed up the block, stepping over trampled
garments, bloodstained debris, and smashed and destroyed
merchandise. She noticed an abandoned soldier's helmet
lying next to a smashed TV. *Good for 'em!* she thought as she
bent over to pick it up like some trophy, but quickly pulled
her hand back, realizing it was soaked in blood.

She gasped for breath as she looked up to see a woman
haulin' ass down the street toward her with an armful of
frozen chickens.

"Baby, don't go up there! Them soldiers is locking up
everybody they can catch," the woman informed her as she
strained with her arms full.

"Ain't you comin' from there?" Delores asked, wanting to
say, *Why you ain't locked up?*

"They ain't catch me, baby," the woman said with a re-
bellious chuckle as she continued home with her chickens,
thinkin' about dinnertime.

Well, they ain't catchin' me neither, thought Delores.

As she turned the corner onto Springfield a crowd of people
were gathered in a circle around a man lying on the ground.
Delores walked up a little closer, maneuvering through the
crowd, getting close enough to see that the man lying on the
ground was clutching a bottle of Thunderbird wine. People
were trying to identify him but his face was beaten badly
and drenched in blood, making him unrecognizable to the
community.

"Is he dead?" a small, girlish voice ventured from the crowd.

"Who is he?" asked an old woman in a housecoat looking for her son whom she hadn't seen or heard from since the riots broke out.

"He don't look like he's movin' to me," said an old homeless man known as Willie.

"Call an ambulance," shouted Delores to Willie.

"An ambulance! Shit, girl, you think an ambulance gonna come over here if we calling for 'em?" questioned some chick wearing a fire-red wig, fire-red high heels, and a skintight dress to match. *Look at this broad, looking like Ms. Kitty from Gunsmoke*, thought Delores to herself as she smiled at the woman.

"I think this nigga just drunk," someone added.

"Or dead," chimed Ms. Kitty.

"Or both," said Willie, shaking his head, as the crowd burst into laughter and began to disperse in different directions, leaving Delores standing alone, still staring down at the man's lifeless body. She had never seen a dead body, at least not in the middle of the street, and she wondered how people could find such a sight funny.

She turned away as she saw the small grocery store on the corner she knew all too well. It seemed untouched, just sitting there in the midst of all the rubble and surrounding destruction.

Sirens wailed, gunshots rang, and people could be heard shouting and cursing as they looted the streets. Yet the store sat serenely and intact by itself as if it were in another place. She made her way across the street and closer to the dark and deserted store. She saw signs plastered over the windows that read **Black Owned**.

No they didn't! Delores stared in disbelief. *Black Owned. How can it say that?* Delores knew better. She knew all too well that the store wasn't black owned. Everybody knew that. She knew the old white man who owned it, Mr. Reilly. She knew how he smelled when he leaned too close to her and how his yellowed teeth sickened her when he leered at her openly, like she was a piece of meat. He knew how hard her mother worked and how she always had to scrape and scramble to pay her weekly grocery bill, but still Mr. Reilly would take every opportunity to humiliate her whenever she was as much as a day late in payment.

"Do you think I run a charity, girl?" he would ask, addressing her as if she weren't a woman.

"No, sir, Mr. Reilly. I have asked you before to address me with the same respect I address you," her mother would reply.

Mrs. Murphy was a proud black woman. She knew that for the sake of keeping food on her table she would have to swallow a little pride now or swallow nothing later. Little did she know that Delores would have rather starved.

"You people don't know the meaning of responsibility," he had spat on more than one occasion.

"I am not 'you people,' Mr. Reilly."

"You're all alike, beggin' bastards," he could be heard mumbling as he wrapped her order.

Delores remembered it like yesterday as she trembled with a rage inside her as she read the sign again and her head began to spin. **Black Owned.**

Behind her, people dashed along as broken glass shattered, policemen shouted through bullhorns off in the distance, and sirens sounded, creating the backdrop for the maddening situation she felt herself in. She looked around on the ground frantically, the anger mounting by the minute until she found a large rock, so large she needed both hands to lift it. Hoisting the rock over her head with all the strength she could muster, she threw the rock through the door, shattering the bottom half of the glass just enough for her to scurry in. Looking around for something to smash, she ran for the cooler where she knew Mr. Reilly kept all the dairy products and started smashing cartons of eggs. Then she picked up a Snickers bar and bit into it, giggling like a lunatic. With candy all over her mouth and chin, it was that moment that she knew how it felt to be free.

Looking around for something to drink, her eyes landed on a bottle of charcoal fluid. She stared at the label with the picture of flaming steaks and she imagined the store burning, in flames. She tore off the cap and doused everything with the entire bottle of fluid, forgetting about her thirst. Grabbing another bottle, she did the same, until she had emptied every bottle of charcoal fluid she could find in the store. She looked for matches, finding some behind the counter. She lit the first match, but the deep breaths she was taking blew it right out. Striking another match, she held it to a paper bag, which she used as a torch to set small fires in the store. She backed up and staggered through the hole in the door she had come through. She watched the small fires turn to dark clouds of gray smoke as the flames began to leap and dance higher and higher like happy slaves on Juneteenth.

Delores found a spot under a large shade tree and sat down with her knees pulled tightly against her chest as she watched her work. She thought of her mother. She knew she could never go back there. Her mother had raised her in a strict Christian environment. She had taught Delores respect for people and their property. She had taught her love and, most important, the moral value of turning the other cheek. But all it had gotten her mother was a maid's job scrubbing white people's floors. Delores decided if she ever turned the other cheek, it would be the one that the world could kiss. She was seventeen years old.

In 1971, by the time Delores was twenty-one, she had forgotten when she had lost her virginity, but she also had forgotten the last time she went hungry. She was the talk of the town and every young hustler wanted a chance to have her on his tongue. If her innocence had died in the ashes of the riot, her pride, beauty, and cunning were born like the Phoenix, the bird of prey.

Since Delores decided not to go back to her mother's house, she did decide to go with the next best thing, her mother's sister, Gladys, who lived on High Street. Gladys was every bit as wild as her mother was tranquil and as conniving as her mother was honest. She loved Delores with all the love reserved for her sister, who had rejected her.

Her home was an after-hours spot in Brick Towers Apartments. She sold everything from wine to weed, chicken to pussy, but never her own.

"Child, these niggas in the street don't sell enough dope or pimp enough ass to buy out this gold mine I got," she would say when the question came up. Not a big woman, but well proportioned and well intact for a woman in her forties, Gladys was admired as well as respected, and Delores took to her like a magnet. Gladys loved Delores and wasn't about to shelter her from what the real world was really about. She didn't like Delores's decision to leave home so young. The girl still needed grooming, still needed a watchful eye, and Gladys was determined to mold Delores. She wanted her only niece to be resilient enough to survive, yet feminine enough to enjoy what God gave her. So, Gladys didn't stop Delores from being who she wanted to be. She only warned her about who she could become.

"Dee Dee, you see her over there?" asked Gladys, calling Delores by her nickname. "Not the one in the green, the one in the blue. Yeah, her. Honey, let me tell you, child, she was Ms. It just a few months ago 'cause she used to mess with this ol' fine ass nigga named Man. That nigga coulda' had the world. He had so much money, it ain't make no sense. He sold that horse up and down this block, but he went and got fucked up on his own shit. Before you know it, he robbin', stealin', breakin' in motherfuckers' shit. Even had Ms. Ol' It shooting that mess up her arm, and before you know it, he had her out there sellin' her ass, so he could get that monkey off his back. Then, he go and OD and leave Ms. It with nothin' but a jones. Now, she out here trickin' anything for chump change tryin' to keep the shakes off."

Just then a lady carrying a baby with two small children following close behind walked up on the house.

"Hi, Ms. Gladys," said the girl.

"Hey, baby, how you today?" asked Ms. Gladys as she and Delores sat on the porch catching a breeze.

"I'm fine," the girl replied, passing by.

"Now that's Bernadette. Smart girl, just stupid. Every decision that child make, be wrong. And every sour man she mess with leave her with nothing but sweet-sounding words and a belly filled up. The girl twenty-two years old and she got five kids and Mr. Sam said he think she pregnant again."

Delores learned everybody's mistakes, through gossip. And even though she made a few of her own, her head was on straight. Straight enough to steer her way clear of life's misfortunes, thanks to Gladys. Her looks and vivaciousness kept her in all the latest designs, but her mind kept her out of all the classic pitfalls.

It was the end of August at the yearly summer block party when she first met him. She saw the tall jet-black brother in the Army-green uniform and she just knew she had him all figured out. The way he watched her, he was just like all the rest of the gawkers on her long list of admirers, except his suit had him at the bottom. Besides, the last time she had seen a soldier, Newark was a war zone. So, his first impression drew scorn instead of interest.

Al Green, or Grits, as everyone who knew him jokingly called him, was booming out the DJ's speakers. When the song ended, Mr. Army approached her, just as Marvin Gaye's "What's Going On" began playing.

"Hey there, mama, I say what is really going on?"

Delores looked him up and down with feigned indifference, feigned because despite his uniform, he was one fine-ass black man.

"Why? You gonna arrest me or somethin'?" asked Delores with a capital A for attitude.

He flashed a perfect Colgate smile and laughed, giving her a tingle at the base of her spine from the sound of his voice.

"I might, if I can't get the next dance," he replied, and as if on cue the DJ played Candi Stanton's "Victim." It was her favorite song, but she wasn't about to tell him that. Instead, she folded her arms across her breasts and looked away so she could lie without looking in his soft baby browns.

"I don't like this song."

"Come on, sugar. You expect me to believe that when your body is sayin' something else?"

She shot him a look and let him know he was right but she resented the fact that he saw through her facade so easily.

"You know, I've been around the world twice, so any flavor there is, I've had a double dip, but ain't nothing like you ever come 'cross my plate."

She looked him up and down again, but the truth was he had her open, just like that, and her heart had already been softened by his satiny charm. She knew she was being gamed. She wasn't a dummy. Yet still, she liked it. Her young ego felt appeased to know she was being judged by worldwide standards, so she couldn't help but crack a smile at that one.

"Ahh, she smiles. So, now can I have your name?"

"No," Delores simply stated.

"No?" he questioned her back, wondering who this chick was.

"No, but you can have this dance," she said, looking into his eyes.

He grabbed her hand and led her to the middle of the street. Her feet never touched the ground. Song after song they moved as if they were dancing on clouds to a rhythm of one heartbeat. Delores melted, giving in to the sweet sense of security, wrapped in his strong arms. She didn't know his name and she didn't need to. All she knew was that she was ready and willing to abandon her security net and go full throttle into what was unknown with this man she'd only known a few moments. It wouldn't be long after the song ended that he'd know her name and she would moan his passionately . . . and it all came down like a jones.

The next couple of weeks for Delores were filled with a love only the ghetto could create. A desperate intense feeling of love that made Delores wake up every morning singing and go to sleep at night humming, enveloped in the arms of her soldier. She moved into his one-room boardinghouse apartment after convincing the ever-religious, always-nosy landlady, Mrs. Tendrell, that they were married.

"I don't know what them other folks do with they homes. They a bunch of whorehouses and gamblin' dens, but as for me and my house, I serve the Lord up in here and I don't want no evil do-mongers up in here," she said to them the day they were moving in.

Delores and her soldier shared a secret snicker for their innocent deception, laughing and mocking Mrs. Tendrell many a time. They were constant companions, gambling at Gladys's, drinking corn liquor until they came home staggering with laughter, then falling out on their three-legged bed, which Delores had put a paint can under to hold up the frame. They'd make wild and passionate love. His wasn't rough, just hard, long, intense strokes, up and down and kissing, like their lips and tongues were meant to be in each other's mouth. As he turned her over on her stomach, he gently placed himself back inside her. He humped her faster and faster, flowing through her in and out, on his knees, flat again, up and down. Then he turned her back around, legs clinging to his back as they stimulated one another into an orgasmic bliss.

Everything was perfect.

But the end came as unexpected and abruptly as the beginning. Even as she thought back to the day, in the midst of her present-day luxury and security, she longed for the cramped boardinghouse room and the love it contained. The tears moistened her cheeks and it felt like an invisible hand gripped her heart as she remembered that rainy afternoon so long ago.

"Baby, I been thinking," was how he solemnly began. He stood by the bed looking out the one and only window in the room.

"About me?" she flirted, not yet grasping the gravity of his tone.

Her words made him force a smile.

"Always, you," he assured her, then cleared his throat and looked back out the window, unable to face the innocent trust and devotion that represented everything she was to him.

"Baby, you okay?" she asked, beginning to worry.

He didn't answer that question; only silence filled the room.

"If there was anything I didn't plan on for this leave, it was to meet someone like you."

Leave? She questioned the term, but she recognized in the word a certain prior commitment to another life.

"Leave?" she repeated, asking him for clarity.

"Leave days. My tour of duty ended, and after that you get a thirty-day leave. Most people don't call it a leave, but I do."

She couldn't speak. Her mind spun like a top set loose, whirling and whirling around and around. *He can't leave me,* she thought as an ache hit her hard. *Please don't leave me,* she thought, *please don't be leaving.* And just like that the top stopped spinning and so did she. She sat down real calm, as if his words had left her somewhere far away. She just sat real still, holding it all in, holding on as the tears warmed her eyes at the sound of his words. *How could he do this to me. I thought he loved me,* she thought as he walked over to her and kneeled before her as if he were about to propose, only he wasn't and she knew it by the look on his face.

"I—I . . . I know it's hard to hear 'cause this is hard for me to say," he said with tears in his eyes and a pained look on his face, as if his world was more torn than hers. "And I know it'll be even harder to do, but you see, sugar, it's something I gotta do," he tried to explain, almost in a whisper, his voice cracking from the pain he felt trying to explain why it was time he leave the woman he loved with all his heart.

"Why?" she asked as a single teardrop fell from her eye. She was asking why not only of him for leaving, but of herself for loving and of God for allowing her to love. However, it seemed that he was the only one with an answer. He stood back up, his full six-foot-three frame dwarfing her as she sat on the edge of the small, twin-framed bed looking down into her hands clasped tightly in her lap. He sat back down next to her and began.

"I never told you why I went and joined the Army. I never told nobody, not even my own mama, but I guess this is as good a time as any." He chuckled lightly and continued. "I remember the way you looked at me the first time we met, me in my uniform and all. You looked at me like I was crazy. What's a black man doing in the Army is what your eyes said to me, and I liked it. Sound funny me sayin' that, huh?" he asked her as she nodded, not saying a word, just listening. "But, it's true, don't no black man belong in no white man's Army, fightin' and dyin' for no white man's war. But, baby, I ain't join to fight no war for them. I went over there to fight my own war, to fight the war I knew I could never win over here. The war goin' on every day on every black man in America. The war they say don't exist. But, I know it exist, 'cause I been fightin' it my whole life and losin' a little bit every day, losin' my respect, losin' my love, damn near losin' my goddamn mind."

He stood up as silence filled the air and he walked over to the solitary chair in the room and picked up his pack of Kools out his jacket pocket. He pulled one out and lit it.

"A man can lose his mind fightin' an enemy he can't see, gettin' it from every which way and not knowin' where it's comin' from, why or when it's gonna come knock you on your ass again. Every black man you done seen or know done felt that. Only difference, from me and them, is that they confused, they fight the wrong people. They get to thinkin' it's comin' from them, so he start fightin' his woman, start fightin' his kids, start fightin' his brother, even start fightin' with himself. They confused, they mad, they hate, they despise, and then they blood turn to poison and a man can't live like that. So, before I lost everything I got lucky, I figured out who the enemy was and how they was winnin', you just couldn't *see them*." He emphasized his words with his hands as if he were gripping an invisible person. He slowly walked to the window, blowing smoke against the pane with Delores's eyes glued to his back.

"My first time in the bush wasn't nothing. A little spelling recon operation, me and about five others, two was white boys. Them Vietnamese muhfuckers was sure nuff slick. They had tunnels that went everywhere and would come outta the ground like snakes. The first shots I fired in action struck one of those white boys square in the back, then everybody ran for cover. From where I was, I could see the other white boy; he could see me, too. See, baby, they fightin' some war for they president, but I'm fightin' my own. So, when I lifted my M-16 he ain't pay no attention, no attention till it was too late. The look on his face, when the nose of that M-16 swung around and stopped on him . . ." Just then he broke out into a mad liberating laughter, which scared and warmed Delores all at the same time. It was that same laughter she heard come from her own mouth the night she bit into that Snickers bar, then set Mr. Reilly's store on fire. She watched him as he turned around to face her, pretending to hold a gun in his hand.

"He didn't know what was going on, till them slugs ripped through his face like paper . . . just like paper," he said, his words traveling off into a distance as he pictured himself that day in full living color.

"That was my first," he said proudly as he took a long draw on his cigarette, then let the smoke out slowly. "I lost count after fifty-somethin'. Sometimes, I'd mow 'em down in bunches, sometimes one by one, and sometimes I'd get me one while he was sleepin', cut that muhfucker's throat without ever makin' a sound. But you know, I never killed one of them Vietnamese people, except in self-defense. Shit, I see one of them muhfuckers and keep right on about my business, unless they got in the way. But naw, them crackers, they catchin' it out there from me, every chance I get," he said, flicking his cigarette out the window. He walked back over to the bed and sat down next to her, taking her hands into his.

"I . . . I don't expect you to understand it, baby. I just . . . I gotta be where insanity is acceptable, where my anger is legal, you know? Where a black man *can* fight back . . . fight back for every black man lynched, every black woman raped, every black child cold and hungry. I can kill these muhfuckers and come home to you, free. I know it sounds crazy . . ." his voice trailed off to a mumble as Delores just stared at his bowed head.

He probably didn't think she understood, but she did. She understood the need to destroy old ghosts in order to fully face the future. She knew deep inside that he wasn't telling her he was leaving, he was *asking* her to let him go. Delores knew he would stay if she refused. He'd stay and gradually she would come to despise him for allowing anyone to get in the way of his freedom, including her. It was a feeling she had come to value above all else. She also knew that he would come to despise her, if she didn't let him go.

Delores traveled off in the near future to one day . . . their wedding day. She imagined herself in a white flowing gown and her soldier standing so tall and handsome in his uniform. She knew that day would never come. The house they would live in for the rest of their lives would never be built, and the life they would share they would never have, and she resigned herself to the reality of the situation. It was over.

Tears streamed from both of them, silently. She kneeled with him on the floor, took his tear-soaked chin into her hand, and lifted it to look into his eyes. Their last words were hers, "I love you."

They parted at the entrance to Pennsylvania Station in New York City. She watched him disappear from her life in the sea of people moving to and fro through the terminal. She waited until she could no longer see him, then returned to the cab awaiting her.

She never heard from him again. He never wrote, he never came back. She never had the chance to tell him she was pregnant. She never had the chance to tell him he had a son. A son that she named after him, Bernard James, Jr.

CHAPTER THREE

◆

ROBERTO'S PIZZERIA

This court stands in recess for lunch until one o'clock," the judge said, banging his gavel loudly as he stood.

The courtroom hummed with the cacophony of multiple conversations being carried on as people filed out. Michael Glass asked Dutch if he needed to see him before he went to lunch.

"Enjoy," is all Dutch replied. He flashed Glass a reassuring smile. As Glass walked out he noticed that there were a lot of old women in the courthouse. *Unusual for this kind of trial,* he thought to himself. He shrugged them off as probably the mothers of Dutch's many victims hoping and praying for justice. *Not if I can help it, old ladies,* thought Glass with a devilish grin on his face. He walked out, with Dutch walking slowly behind him, taking in the many faces in the crowd until he stopped on one in particular who was still seated in the back of the courtroom. He looked again, placing the familiar face he hadn't seen in years. It was Mrs. Piazza. He smiled sincerely as he approached her.

"Mrs. P, is that you?" Dutch asked, knowing that it was.

"Of course it is. Whazza matter, you tryin' to say I'm

getting old?" Mrs. Piazza asked as she stood up and hugged Dutch tightly.

"You don't look a day older than the day I last saw you," he lied, looking at all the makeup she wore trying to cover the many wrinkles life had dealt over the years. She playfully hit him.

"And you still can't lie, I see," she said to him.

They shared a light chuckle.

"It's been a while. How are you doing?" she asked with lines of concern on her brow.

"When have you known me to worry, huh?" Dutch responded, and she could tell he wasn't worried at all. But she was. "I didn't expect you to be here," he said, happy she was.

"I didn't expect you to be here, either," she joked. "How's your mother?"

"Like you, worrying too much," Dutch answered.

"Things ain't the same, Dutch, not since—" Her voice broke off and Dutch quickly cut in to comfort her.

"Nothing's changed, Mrs. P, trust me, really. Okay?"

Just then, one of Dutch's boys walked up.

"Give me a minute." Dutch spoke in a tone letting the guy know he needed privacy as he turned his back to him and focused on Mrs. Piazza.

"You sure you okay? Can I take you somewhere?"

"No. No, thank you, I'm driving. I just wanted to see, to see if you needed anything," Mrs. Piazza told him.

"You know what I need. One of your old-fashioned Italian feasts, huh? After this is all over, I want some chicken française, fettuccini alfredo, the stewed vegetables with the potatoes, and some of your homemade lasagna. Oh, and of course, a pizza."

They both laughed, but they both knew there'd be no gourmet Italian feast after this, no matter what happened in the courtroom.

"Sure, I'd like that," said Mrs. Piazza, trying to sound convincing.

"It's a date then. Listen, I gotta go, though."

"I know, I know, go ahead. Take care of yourself, Bernard," she said, cutting him off and wishing him a last farewell.

He nodded, and with that, he was off.

As Mrs. Piazza opened the door to her blue Volvo wagon and got in, she stopped short of inserting the key into the ignition. She sat back in the leather interior and peered up at the courthouse that towered above her. She had been here many times over the years, but this was the first time she had felt so dwarfed by the building. It was the first time the courthouse had looked so ominous, despite the afternoon sunlight. When her husband, Roberto, was alive, he himself had been in and out of this building, but always with a smile and a swagger in his step. He never saw a day in jail. But Roberto had died three years ago.

That was the last time she had seen Dutch, at the funeral, and she thought how Dutch over the years had played such a major part in her life. She knew if he were Italian, he wouldn't be on trial for his life, and for the thousandth time, she wished that he was. She always wished that for Dutch because she disliked blacks, not passionately, but passively.

In her eyes, they never amounted to anything, except Dutch. Dutch was different. He had saved her husband's life and her own. Her mind traveled back fifteen years to the day when Roberto had his pizza parlors.

The parlors did well, but the better business took place in the back where Roberto handled Fat Tony's gambling money. Roberto had five parlors in different parts of Newark, all in impoverished areas, so Mrs. Piazza was exposed to the seedy, seething side of the ghetto. Her interactions with blacks were usually with the street element and the drug addicts who sold them everything from kitchen appliances to jewelry, all stolen and very cheap.

Not to mention the young black girls who spat out baby after baby, running scams on the welfare department, getting food stamps, then bringing them to her in exchange for cash; seven dollars for every ten dollars in food stamps. Then there were the little kids who never seemed to go to school and who had no pride in their appearance. They hung around the pizza parlor trying to jig her video machines with paper clips for free games. These were the types of blacks by whom she shaped her opinion of all blacks, and she treated them all the same. This was her idea of equality.

Dutch was one of the young boys who always came to her pizza parlor and hung around. He was a lot like all the rest, except he usually had some money and seemed to have good hygiene habits. She also noticed her husband taking an interest in the little black boy. Roberto would let him sweep the floor and help unload the delivery trucks every Thursday, stuffing the boy with pizza and worldly chat. She, unlike her husband, didn't warm to Dutch's presence, but merely grew accustomed to him being underfoot . . . until that night.

It was a night like any other at closing time. Dutch was sweeping the floor, while Mrs. Piazza was cleaning the counters and utensils. Roberto was balancing the cash register when all of a sudden, a tall black man in a ski mask burst through the front door brandishing a .38 caliber revolver and yelling, "You know what it is! Gimme what I want 'fore you get what you don't!"

Mrs. Piazza froze with a feeling of fear mixed with anger. How dare one of these niggers try to take something from her? How dare he step into her husband's shop and demand anything? But her anger took a backseat to her fear as the gunman pointed the .38 at her, then waved it in the direction of her husband.

"You! Get over there by yo' husband and start takin' off them rings and them chains, NOW!" Mrs. Piazza moved over closer to her husband, quickly removing her many jewels. Dutch stared at the gunman openly. The gunman turned to him. "Who the fuck is you? The monkey or somethin'? Get yo' ass in front of me where I can see you, nigga!"

Dutch stepped over to the counter on the gunman's left, still clutching the broom. The gunman ran up to the cash register and shoved the gun in Roberto's face.

"Okay, you fuckin' wop, put all that money in a bag, real quick, ya dig, and it'll all go down smooth."

Roberto began to fill the bag, never taking his eyes off the gunman. He was trying to find a distinctive mark or tattoo with which to identify the man later, on his own time, but the gloves and mask completely covered up his skin.

"Hurry up!"

Dutch looked at the murder in Roberto's eyes and he knew he had to do something. He looked at the gunman, who continued to keep a close watch on him in case he tried to run. But Dutch was no sprinter. He had already decided what to do by the time Roberto handed the bag to the robber and he began backing toward the door. Just as the gunman was about to make his exit, Dutch spoke up.

"That's not all the money."

Roberto and his wife looked at Dutch with wide-eyed surprise. The gunman stopped dead in his tracks.

"Whut?" he asked, confused, as he glanced down at the bag of money he held. "Whut you say?"

"I said, that ain't all the money. The old wop got a safe in the back," Dutch stated calmly, watching the greed build in the gunman's eyes.

Roberto shot Dutch a look of death. "You little black bastard! I'll kill you! I may not know him, but I swear to God I'm gonna fuckin' kill you!"

Mrs. Piazza looked at her husband, concerned for his blood pressure and bad heart, then coldly stared at Dutch. How could Dutch do that after all her husband had done for him? She couldn't figure it out. She questioned, but it made no sense to her.

"Roberto, why you let the black kid sweep up at the end of the night? He's a moulyan and you got him hanging around like he belongs," she had questioned her husband.

"I like the kid, Miriam. Is that okay with you? He's just a kid, he's harmless," Roberto had responded.

He isn't that fuckin' harmless. He got a nigger in our restaurant about to rob us blind, thought Mrs. Piazza to herself.

The gunman looked at Roberto, then at Dutch, then took a quick glance over his shoulder at the street. He lifted the gun in Roberto's direction, then waved it toward the back.

"You heard the little nigga", he said, smiling like a Cheshire cat. "Let's go in the back, all of us."

Roberto looked at Dutch angrily and Dutch returned his gaze nonchalantly. They all headed to the back with the gunman bringing up the rear. When they reached the storage room, the gunman shoved Mrs. Piazza into the corner and put the gun to Roberto's head. "Where's the safe, lil' man?" he asked Dutch, never taking his eyes off Roberto.

"Bottom drawer of the file cabinet. Snatch the door off and it's right there," Dutch told him.

"Get to it, cracker," the gunman spat as Roberto shot Dutch one last murderous stare, before bending down to open the bottom drawer. When it was removed, it revealed a large safe.

"Bingo!" the gunman hollered happily.

Roberto opened the safe and inside were stacks and stacks of money.

"Cl-clean it out!" the gunman stammered. He'd never seen so much money in his life. He'd only hoped for enough to get high for the night, but the safe appeared to have enough to get high for the rest of his life!

"Thanks, lil' man. You leave wit' me after this!"

He took his attention off Dutch, which was his first and last mistake. Mrs. Piazza saw the gun come out of Dutch's waist before her husband. The gunman never saw it. She started to scream and the little sound that did escape her lips caught the gunman's attention, but before he could turn around . . .

His brains sprayed all over the cabinet and the walls and

on Roberto's dirty white apron. He slumped over dead before he hit the floor. Roberto looked up completely astonished to see the automatic .32 in Dutch's hand and a smile
on his young black face.

"What the fuck?" was all Roberto could stammer out as
Dutch retucked his gun and leaned against the wall calmly.
Mrs. Piazza stared blankly at Dutch. Her heart told her it
was all over, but her mind couldn't compute the chain of
twisting events that had left a dead black man lying at her
feet quickly enough. Just moments before, she would've paid
anything to see Dutch lie in a pool of his own blood. But
now she found herself thanking Mary, mother of Jesus, that
he had been there. No one spoke but Dutch.

"Gimme the keys to the van and I'll take care of the
body," Dutch told Roberto.

Roberto was still too shocked to say anything. He merely
reached into his pocket and handed Dutch the keys.

When Dutch returned, Mrs. Piazza was sitting behind
the counter sipping a cup of black coffee. She had calmed
down by then. It wasn't the blood or even the body that
shook her up. She had seen more than her share of those,
being married to the mob. It was the way this young black
boy had so correctly calculated the situation and moved so
swiftly. Dutch approached the counter and dropped the keys
by her hand.

"Roberto in the back?" he asked politely.

She nodded. It was then that she knew this young black
child was a cold-blooded killer. Only the cold-blooded could
do what he had done and return with the innocence of youth.
As Dutch went toward the back, she called to him.

"Hey," was all she said because she didn't know his name. Dutch turned to face her.

"Thank you." She smiled.

Dutch returned her smile and then disappeared in the back.

Two days later, Dutch was on her front porch. She answered the door to find him standing there.

"Hello, Mrs. Piazza. How are you?"

"Fine, young man, fine. Please, come in," she said, standing aside to allow him to pass. Her husband had invited young Dutch over for dinner and to meet Fat Tony Cerone, to whom the safe and its contents belonged. She walked Dutch into the living room where Tony and Roberto were sitting waiting for dinner. She returned to the kitchen, which was separated from the living room only by a cabinet-counter partition. Roberto stood up to shake Dutch's hand. Fat Tony, who was too fat to get up even if he wanted to, sat through the introduction.

"So, this is him, huh? This is the kid we owe sixty-five thousand to?" Fat Tony asked through teeth clenched tight around an equally fat cigar.

"What's your name, kid?"

"Dutch."

"Dutch? Strange name for a black kid; how'd you get a name like Dutch?" Tony asked.

Dutch just shrugged his shoulders as if he didn't know, but he knew it just wasn't important. Young as he was, he realized he was in the presence of power and knew the potential of such a situation.

He'd learned from Roberto that Italians may be clannish and not particularly fond of his kind, but he knew they could recognize a thoroughbred at first sight.

"Sit down, Dutch. Take a load off," Roberto suggested, gesturing to the love seat across from Fat Tony.

"How old are you, Dutch?"

"Fourteen."

"Fourteen, huh? When I was fourteen, I had a BB gun, a hard dick, and both were shootin' blanks," Tony said and they all shared a laugh.

"I guess times have changed since then," Dutch replied, wearing what would become his trademark smile.

"Yeah, I guess so. Listen, I want you to know I really appreciate what you did for me," Tony said as his expression lost its humorous touch and became serious. "But, of course, I wouldn't have to be here if you hadda kept your mouth shut, huh?" Tony concluded, but Dutch didn't answer because he knew Tony had answered his question himself.

"So, let me ask you somethin', Dutch. What were you thinking about when you just fuckin' blurted out to the fuckin' guy about my safe, huh? What the hell was on your mind jeopardizin' my fuckin' money for fuckin' pizza money, huh?" Tony was huffing from the energy he expended, so he sat back, puffed his cigar, looked at Dutch, and waited for a response.

"I like Roberto," Dutch simply stated.

"You what?" Fat Tony asked as if he didn't hear Dutch the first time.

"I like Roberto," Dutch repeated.

"Izzat so? Well, what would've happened if the fuckin' guy didn't take your suggestion, huh, then what? Suppose he hadn't believed you and ran out leaving you to deal with the fact that Roberto trusted you and you fuckin' betrayed that trust, then what? You think Roberto would've liked you then?"

"To me, it wasn't just pizza money. It belonged to Roberto, and since I consider Roberto a friend, stealing from him was like stealing from me, and any man is gonna do what they gotta do when what belongs to him is threatened. So, I did what I had to do, but if I woulda been wrong, then we wouldn't be having this conversation and I'd probably be dead," Dutch explained as Fat Tony just sat there looking at him like he was crazy.

"You afraid to die?" Tony asked as he paused for a moment, intensely studying Dutch.

"You askin' me am I afraid to die or am I afraid of you?" questioned Dutch as he stared Fat Tony in his eyes, never blinking, never looking away.

"Whichever one's more appropriate to the question," Fat Tony responded with a smirk as he looked at Roberto.

"Then no," Dutch replied, his eyes locked on Fat Tony.

Cigar smoke drifted between the two and the eye contact was broken. Tony dumped his ashes in the ashtray as he looked back at Dutch.

"But," Dutch continued, "I do respect you, Mr. Cerone."

Dutch stood up and held out his hand to Tony. Tony looked up at the small, black hand extended to him, then up into the eyes of the young man it belonged to. *This kid's gotta future,* he thought to himself.

After a few lingering moments he placed his hand in Dutch's and grasped it firmly.

"I like you, kid. You got balls."

"Dinner's ready!" Mrs. Piazza called out. It had been ready for over five minutes, but she had waited and listened to every word and saw every gesture between the men and the boy. She thought about her childless womb, and how she wished it had been filled with a son like Dutch. That was the first time she wished Dutch was Italian.

Brought back to reality by a bunch of rowdy young black kids walking past with a handheld radio blaring, she placed the key in the ignition of her Volvo.

"Moulies," she remarked and pulled off.

CHAPTER FOUR

♦

LOCK DOWN

Craze looked up from the blunt he was rolling in his money-green 911 Porsche Turbo to see Mrs. Piazza's blue Volvo drive by as she left the courthouse. Dutch had Craze outside in the parking lot watching everything and everybody. Dutch wanted to know who came and left the courthouse, what time, who they was with and what they was driving. Craze understood the importance of his assignment, but that didn't make it any less boring. He needed the weed to break the monotony. And his Dutch-style Coronas and Scarface CD.

He looked around self-consciously as he lit the blunt thinking how Dutch felt about his people and drug use. Dutch didn't get high and was so tight on his people about using drugs, Craze thought he might even implement a piss test or some shit. Craze knew the golden meaning of getting c.r.e.a.m. *Don't get high on your own supply,* but he sold or rather oversaw the sale of heroin, not weed, for Dutch's organization.

It had been years since he had actually touched the brown powder that gave him the ability to retire at twenty-eight. But to Dutch, drugs were drugs, no matter what kind.

"How many crackheads you know started drugs wit' weed?" Dutch would ask in anger whenever he found Craze's stash or caught him smoking.

"Nigga, you sayin' I'm a crackhead?" Craze would shoot back.

"Shit, neither was G-Money at first," referring to *New Jack City*. "And you know what happened to him," Dutch would jokingly add.

"Muhfuck you, nigga. You can't kill me. You'd go crazy without me, baby. That shit would be like Tony without Manny, Bonnie without Clyde, the Rat Pack without Sammy and shit. Just wouldn't be right, nigga."

Dutch knew he was right. Not only because Craze was so instrumental in Dutch's organization, but because the two men were like brothers. They had grown up from being babies together, even rode in the same baby carriage together. Craze's mother died when he was only eight and he went to stay with his aunt. Up until then, if you saw one, you saw the other. Craze, aka Christopher Shaw, had gotten his nickname just trying to keep up with Dutch. Dutch's craziness was psychotic and only those who were truly close to him knew the risks he took. But Craze's insanity was worn on his sleeve like stripes. Everybody knew Chris was crazy, so there was no need to call him Chris anymore. Crazy shortened to Craze over the years and he eventually mellowed out. Actually he hadn't mellowed, but everybody felt he had because he had fewer and fewer opportunities to prove his nickname.

But seeing Mrs. Piazza again after so many years stimulated Craze's mind with vivid pictures of how he and Dutch got in the position to be attempting what they were now planning to carry out.

As Mrs. Piazza's taillights faded into traffic, he thought back to the first time he saw her at the pizza parlor. He saw her as a nasty old bitch who was always running them off from her video games if they hung around too long without buying anything. He hated Roberto, too, because of the way he handed him his change whenever he did buy something. He would half throw it or half drop it in Craze's hands, like he was contagious with color.

That's why he questioned Dutch whenever Dutch would be sweeping the floor or helping Roberto unload trucks.

"Man, why you always doin' shit for that muhfucker? You know he don't even like us?"

But, even at such a young age, Dutch was able to see an opportunity in even the most insignificant situations.

"I don't give a fuck about him. He's just a pizza man. It's who he fuckin' wit', and you don't hang around shit like that without something falling your way."

"Well, damn, you can at least get a couple of dollars or somethin', like some free video games, fuckin' somethin'. You damn near workin' for free," Craze complained.

"Naw, man, that's what he expects, some little petty-ass black kid starvin' for chicken change. Naw, when you dealin' with cats like him who outweigh you, always keep 'em off balance. 'Cause then the weight don't mean shit to a muh-fucka wit' leverage." Dutch would always philosophically explain shit.

He had always been smart. In school—whenever he and Craze actually went—he would ace tests without even studying and devour books while Craze chased girls and fought over candy money. But it got to a point when Dutch got bored and graduated himself from school at the age of twelve. For Craze, school didn't matter to him one way or the other. So when Dutch stopped going, so did he. While Craze ran the streets doing the things ghetto kids do, Dutch put in time gaining Roberto's confidence.

Craze didn't know what to do with himself, and his small life felt monotonous. He was bored with stealing cars, joyriding, and ducking the truancy officer, who had placed Craze on a 9:30 P.M. curfew.

As he sat in his bedroom window smoking a cigarette one night, he heard Dutch's bird-call from outside. He looked down and saw Dutch.

"Yo! Come here! I gotta show you somethin'," Dutch hollered.

Craze was out the window and down the fire escape as if it was the normal way to exit the premises. Moving like a cat, he jumped down onto the ground and walked over to Dutch.

"What up?" Craze asked.

"Just come on."

They walked around the corner and Craze saw Roberto's white van sitting halfway down the block.

"You finally got smart and robbed his old ass, huh?" Craze asked as he lit another cigarette.

Dutch just looked at him and wondered why he would think that after everything he'd been trying to tell him.

"Yo, Craze, I love you like a brother, but once I open this door and show you what's inside, ain't no turning back, nigga. You either wit' me or go on and walk away now," Dutch solemnly declared.

Craze looked Dutch in the face and in his eyes. He had never heard such words from him before. He considered Dutch his brother, his heart. If he didn't die for the mother-fucker, he would certainly die with him, and he knew Dutch knew this. So, for Dutch to say what he just said, Craze knew whatever was in the van was nothing like he had seen before. His stomach knotted at the thought and tightened as he spoke.

"Yo, Duke, you know how we get down. You and I, do or die, you ain't got to tell me to walk nowhere," Craze stated with all the sincerity his heart could muster.

Dutch looked him in the eyes and, when he was satisfied, nodded and opened the back doors of the van. He and Craze stepped up into the van and Craze saw a long, bulky object lying between two garbage bags. Dutch snatched back the top-layer garbage bag to reveal the dead gunman. Craze took one look and threw up all over the inside of the van.

"Damn, nigga! We got enough to clean up wit'out yo' ass addin' to it!" Dutch told him over Craze's bowed head. For years after, Dutch stayed in his ass, always teasin' Craze about his first sight of a dead body.

"Damn, nigga, took one look at that shit and his whole ass-hole turned inside out!" Dutch would say among the trusted.

After Craze emptied his stomach, he turned back to the body in amazement. It was the first time he had ever seen a dead body, but it wouldn't be the last.

"What the fuck happened to him?" Craze finally got the wind to ask.

"Never mind. We need a whole lot of cinderblocks and some rope," Dutch said, looking like they needed to find that shit right now.

They ran through neighboring backyards, tearing down clotheslines along the way until they found some cinder-blocks in a vacant lot to carry back to the van. When there were enough blocks, Dutch told Craze to drive while he tied the blocks to the clotheslines and secured the lines to the dead body.

"Go to Weequahic Park cross town," Dutch directed from the back.

"Why you want to go all the way over there with them police they got and shit?"

"Will you drive?" Dutch asked, looking at Craze, questioning why he was being questioned.

It was a long and dangerous way to cross town to that side. Newark police were keen on stolen cars. They knew the young car thieves running around and Craze knew they knew him. So, he took the safest, most direct route, Elizabeth Avenue, straight out. The trip was tense but uneventful. He pulled into a secluded area of the park near the lake and pulled over.

"Help me drag this muhfucker to the water," Dutch told Craze.

Craze jumped out the driver's seat and made his way to the back of the van. Dutch already had the back door open. They began to struggle with the body, but they weren't strong enough to drag it out of the van.

"Damn, this muhfucker's heavy," Dutch huffed.

"Yeah, he is," Craze agreed. "Untie the cinderblocks," he suggested, wondering how the fuck they were supposed to carry the motherfucker all tied to cement and shit.

He and Dutch first carried the cinderblocks to a wooded area near the edge of the lake, then came back for the body.

It was still heavy, but they managed to drag it over to the cinderblocks and reattach them. Then they rolled the body to the water and carried it out a bit as it began to sink into liquid darkness. The two boys watched as the body quickly sank to its watery grave. Dutch looked at himself, then at Craze, and saw they were covered with blood and sweat.

"Take off your shirt and go get those garbage bags out the van. Make sure ain't no blood in the van. If it is, try and wipe it up wit' your shirt," Dutch told him.

Within minutes, all the contents of the van were piled in a clearing in the woods. Dutch set the pile on fire and watched as it was reduced to ashes. Then he and Craze returned to the van and drove off.

For the next three days, Craze was worried sick. He hadn't seen Dutch and neither had Ms. Delores, who, unlike Craze, wasn't worried a bit.

"Bernard can take care of hisself," was all she said, then hung up the phone in his ear.

Various scenes flashed through his mind about where Dutch could be. On the bottom of the lake next to the body they dumped or on the run from Roberto and God knows who else, like the police. The only good sign was there was no mention anywhere in the paper of any body or bodies found and there wasn't anything in there about Dutch getting arrested.

Craze, through his own personal contact, learned the identity of the dead man he had buried in Lake Weequahic. He was a local drug addict named Chester. Chester's sister was one of Craze's many young conquests. He had been pestering her about letting him hold her pop's handgun.

"Boy, is you crazy? You ain't gonna get me killed. My

daddy will go crazy. Besides, Chester took it and ain't been home in damn near a week," she said as Craze pushed her head back down into his lap.

A light came on, though, as she was gunnin' him. *Chester, that's where I saw them old-ass Pro-Keds before.* He remembered them on the dead man's feet. He hadn't thought of it at the time, but it came through crystal clear now that Chester's sister mentioned it. He felt funny to have her giving him head after having gotten rid of what was left of her brother, and he felt the vague sense of superiority you feel when you know the answer to the question that is perplexing to others.

"He'll turn up," he said with a slight smirk, amused at the hidden meaning behind his words.

"He better. My father gonna kill that boy one of these days."

So, he knew where the body was, but where was Dutch? That was his last thought that night before drifting off to sleep, only to be awakened in the middle of the night with the answer to his question. He heard the familiar bird call as if it was a dream, and at first he thought he was dreaming until he heard it again.

Dutch.

He hopped up and was down the fire escape before he was dressed.

"Yo, nigga, where the fuck you been?" His tone was full of worry.

"Man, I'm sayin'. I ain't never killed no body before. I ain't know what to do with myself. So, I figured I had better lay in the cut until I knew what was what."

"I know who he is, too," Craze announced cryptically, finally knowing something.

"Who?"

"Chester."

"Chester?" Dutch repeated, thinking hard.

"Chester, Sharice brother."

"Oh, dope-fiend-ass Chester! Always sellin' his people shit. Word?" replied Dutch.

"Word. You seen Roberto?" Craze asked with dollar signs in his eyes. Not only had he been worried about Dutch, he was also worried about the reward he knew Roberto would pay for such a job well done.

"Yeah," was all Dutch replied.

"And?" Craze asked impatiently.

"And everything's everything. He let me come over his house for dinner to meet Fat Tony."

"Aw, man, word?!" Craze's eyes bulged. He knew Fat Tony was a powerful man in the crime family. He knew they were going to get paid now. "What he give you?"

"Nothin'," replied Dutch

"Huh?"

"I said nothin'. I ain't ask for nothin', he ain't give me nothin'," said Dutch, knowing it was driving Craze mad.

"Man, do you know what you did? What we did? Muh-fuckers make livings off of shit like this and you ain't ask for nothin'?" asked Craze disbelievingly, throwing his hands up in disgust. *This nigga is really taking this working for free shit too far.* Craze paced back and forth in a frenzy, calling Dutch any and everything he could think of while Dutch just leaned against the wall watching him.

"Finished?"

"Naw, I'm just catching my breath, you stupid muh-fucker," Craze retorted.

"But I did get a connect. A chop shop," said Dutch with a grin on his face.

"A chop shop?" questioned Craze, answering for himself.

They had been stealing cars all their lives as long as they could remember, but they never knew no chop shop. Craze could see how valuable this connect could be, but he still wasn't convinced.

"He put me on to a chop shop down North Newark. They don't take nothing but Porsches and Corvettes, so you know they hittin' niggas off for them shits."

Craze just eyed Dutch. *You mean to tell me that's all you got, a chop shop connect?* Dutch could have done better, but Craze figured this would have to do. It was better than nothing.

"Trust me, baby boy, for Tony to even give us that says a lot. I could be floating facedown right now, ya dig? But, since I ain't I'll see Tony again one day, on his level, and I promise you . . . we'll never look back."

Craze and Dutch had been working through Dutch's newfound connect for about seven months. They had even started to take other car thieves to the chop shop for a cut but never gave up their contact. The money was good for two fourteen-year-olds. For that matter, it was good for a grown man.

Dutch had assembled a young team of raiders from all over Newark. One-eyed Roc from Prince Street, Qwan from down Bergen, Puerto Rican Angel, a girl from Dayton Street, Zoom from Grafton, and Shock from Seventeenth Avenue, all of whom were under fifteen years old, and Dutch was boss.

They put together routes as far north as Connecticut, as far south as Virginia, and as far west as Ohio. The only trouble they had was when Zoom got caught in Ohio and did six months. Dutch kept his commissary flowing for that bid. Everybody got minibikes and baby Ninja street bikes and gained names for themselves. Older car thieves tried to pressure them for their connect. But these young wolves were far from timid and seldom unarmed.

It was here when Chris began to transform into Craze, or rather Crazy. In fact, he was one of the first to ever pull a carjacking in Newark before the federal laws. Because of the nature of their connect, they never averaged fewer than four or five cars a week. BMW, Mercedes, Corvette, and other luxury cars had the latest in security technology, but it did nothing to deter the appetite of the young band of raiders.

Craze sat back in the plush leather interior of his Porsche and nodded at the accuracy of Dutch's words. Twelve years later, and they still hadn't looked back. Even the present situation hadn't completely stopped their shine, because Dutch had one more trick up his sleeve, and Dutch had seldom been wrong, except once, Port Newark.

Port Newark was a large area that sat on the water. It was the size of a small town where big cars from all over the world were delivered on big ships. The entire area was sectioned off according to make. There were Toyotas, Hondas, Nissans, Mercedes Benzes, BMWs, and Chevrolets. The list went on and on. Every car manufactured sat at the port behind barbed-wire fences. Each lot had at least 150 cars of assorted models.

City police rarely came through the port because the dock had its own security force. The armed security guards

drove around the large port vigilantly watching for any un-
authorized movement. They had to because the port was a
car thief's heaven. Young raiders would drool at the mere
mention of the port but never attempted a heist. Security
was too tight, tight like fish pussy, and that's waterproof.

"Word?" said Shock, expressing interest as the whole
clique gathered before Dutch.

"Fuck we gonna do, rob a bank?" Angel asked sarcastically.

"No, the port."

"Port Newark? How the hell we suppose to do that?" Qwan
questioned.

"Because, I been watchin' them. They slippin'. They
think they untouchable and they startin' to relax. See, four
months ago when I first started scoping the shit, I timed the
security cars. They was coming in circling every five to seven
minutes, then last month they not showing up for say ten
to fifteen minutes, and the last couple of nights, these guys
been coming through like every twenty to thirty minutes.
They even stop and eat. Now keep in mind they done cut
back and it's only two cars to a shift."

The young clique sat thoughtfully, contemplating the
possibilities and the risk.

"Hell yeah! Yo, fuck it, why not? Shit, I'm wit' it."

"Nigga, you wit' anything," Qwan said to Craze.

"Naw naw, this could work," Angel said. "They ain't ex-
pectin' no shit like this right now."

"It could, but how?" asked Shock.

"First of all, we gonna need at least six more heads
'cause if we gonna lick, we might as well make this shit
count. Other than that, we need a blowtorch and some

wire cutters for the fence and the parking barrier. Angel, we gonna get you a pair of fire-red fuck-me pumps and a skirt the size of a napkin," Dutch said, his eyes filled with a playful lust.

All the guys hooted and called to Angel in a teasing way, but Angel didn't find it funny at all. She had the young blossoming body of a *Playboy* centerfold, yet the burgeoning potential of a dyke, which was still unknown to her young conscious mind.

"Fuck you, Dutch. Why we can't put the skirt on Roc? He look more bitch than me," Angel sneered.

"Fuck you, bitch," Roc shot back. He was the quiet before the storm next to Dutch. In the end, Roc would prove to be the deadliest of them all.

"Fuck wit' me," Angel challenged him.

"I'm sayin', y'all gonna play games or is we gonna get this paper?" Dutch asked as no one spoke. "Now dig, Angel, you and Craze are gonna be in the front car. Y'all gonna be parked right at the curb after you enter the port. I want y'all to front like you fighting. Angel, make sure you flash ass 'cause we all know security guards don't get no pussy, 'cause if they did, they wouldn't have night jobs."

Everyone laughed, and Dutch winked at Angel. Angel gave him the middle finger but cracked Dutch a little smile.

"What if they don't bite?" asked Craze.

"Then we dead," stated Dutch. "That's why the second car has to pull over to give us enough time to get in the BMW lot, so make it look good, Craze." Craze nodded in understanding.

"As for the rest of us, we'll be in another parked car behind the lot in the dead end. We ain't gettin' nothing but

BMWs, 'cause the Chevrolet lot got too much shit to be runnin' around lookin' for Corvettes, so strictly Beemers. We gonna need time after the first car pass, I figure three minutes top to snap the fence and blowtorch a hole wide enough in the barrier to get out of. Once we in, we out. Keys sittin' in the ignition, plastic still on the seats."

"Damn, fourteen BMWs. How much is that?" Qwan asked wistfully, daydreaming about cream.

"My man told me he'd give us ten grand for coupes and fifteen for sedans, so you do the math," Dutch replied.

"So, when we gonna do it?" Craze inquired, already calculating that the take would be no less than $140,000 on the coupe end alone.

"Wednesday night," Dutch announced as everyone started counting the days. It was a Saturday.

Four days later, they pulled off of Highway 1&9 and headed toward the port. Dutch checked his watch. It was 9:10 P.M. He wanted to drive through once to get his bearings and locate the cop cars. He pulled over before he reached the entrance to the port. Craze pulled up beside him with Angel in his car. Roc was riding with Shock and a few heads. And Zoom and the Zoo Crew were behind him.

"Go on, get Roc and Shock in position and then you and Angel get your show started. Roc, you and Shock find a spot to hide until we get there. Zoom and the Zoo Crew can stay with me. Don't fuck up," Dutch directed.

Craze nodded and drove off. Dutch just watched them as the taillights of the Delta 88 Craze was driving made a left turn into the port. He waited a few minutes then pulled off heading the same way as Craze.

He saw the squad car and checked his watch: 9:16 P.M.

He didn't know whether it was the first or the second squad car until he pulled into the dead-end road directly behind the BMW lot and saw the second. *It's 9:25 P.M. That's seven minutes,* he thought to himself. That was a lot closer than the last time he checked on them, which was Monday night, but still a safe amount of time between the two. Everyone got out of the cars and stayed low, creeping around the BMW lot. Dutch had Qwan stay in the Cherokee because Qwan was one of the best drivers and Dutch wanted to be prepared just in case they had to bail out.

Off in the distance he saw the taillights of the Delta 88. He could barely see Angel and Craze, just images that could be bodies of anyone. About that time, Roc and Shock crept up on him.

"Whut up?" Shock asked, but Dutch didn't answer.

They waited as Craze saw the headlights of the second car slowly approaching.

"Here they come, baby girl," Craze whispered to Angel, and she went into her act.

"Fuck you, *puta*! Fuck you! *No me toque.*" She swung wildly at Craze, who ducked and grabbed her by the waist, pushing her up against the car. By that time, the squad car was in full view of them.

"The hell is that all about?" the middle-aged white man asked his equally pale partner.

"Lovers' quarrel," shrugged his passenger, "fuck 'em," he continued lazily, taking a hit off a joint before passing it to the driver. The driver took the joint but almost dropped it in his lap when he saw Angel half fall to the ground, revealing nothing but a pair of pink panties fitting tightly around her firm, thick ass.

"God damn, did you see that?" the driver exclaimed, his dick instantly hard.

"Man, with an ass like that, I'd be fightin' too," his partner commented, taking the joint back from him and putting it out. "Back up, man. Maybe we can help and be thanked at the same time," he added, looking over his shoulder.

Craze had almost lost hope until he saw their brake lights come on and the car begin to back up.

"They backin' up, they backin' up," he whispered to Angel.

"Hell yeah! Hell yeah! Yo, let's go," Dutch exclaimed, whispering his words.

Dutch, Shock, and Roc went forward to the barbed-wire fence with the blowtorch and wire cutters. They were in full view if anyone passed, but no one did. Roc quickly snapped through the fence and tore away an entrance.

"Hurry up," Dutch ordered, firmly but calmly, looking toward Craze and the guards as Roc and Shock lit the blowtorch to work on the metal barrier.

The security guards had managed to separate Angel and Craze, each guard holding one of them. Angel was still yelling and cursing as the guard held his arms around her waist, pretending to restrain her. She pretended to reach for Craze to hit him, every time bending forward and pressing her ass against the guard's crotch until she felt his penis harden.

"*Tu eres un enfermo!* Get off of me!" Angel yelled, swinging on the guard.

The other guard let go of Craze and tried to assist his partner, while Roc and Shock worked the blowtorch on the last piece of the barrier. Dutch waved for the rest of the crew and they scurried over. Dutch had hand-picked eight well-known car thieves to assist him and his crew.

"Don't forget, nothing but sedans," Dutch reminded them as they hurried through the gate. He was the last to go through as he looked out over the lot, which was the size of a football field.

It was like a car thief's heaven seeing all those different-colored and different-shaped BMWs sitting there, waiting to be driven away. With the keys in all the cars' ignitions, three dudes had already pulled out by the time Dutch made it to a piss-gold 740il. He looked back just in time to see the second guard's car lights come into full view, flashing, speeding toward the lot. Dutch had misjudged the second car; he had misjudged time and it would cost him.

"Damn, get the fuck outta here," he yelled to the others as he hopped into the 740. Not everybody had time to get to a car of their own, so members of the clique were doubling down and tripling up in whatever was in motion.

Only seven cars made it out. Dutch could've left first, but he positioned himself to be the last car, the sacrifice car. He floored the 740, leaving dust in the air as he tried to make it to the hole in the fence. He zoomed right by Angel and Craze as the security guards looked up in surprise.

"What the hell? Come on!" yelled the security guard as he let go of Angel. The two guards ran for their car, pulling their guns to join the chase.

Qwan, unable to see the security guard's car traveling east as he was traveling south, rammed right into the passenger side of the guard's car. Qwan jumped out and ran, only to be apprehended a few hundred yards away from his parked but still running car.

With that scene in front of him, Dutch stopped short and hit reverse in haste. He spun the car around in a smooth 360 and headed toward the rear of the lot as the second guard car took a security road at the rear of the lot to cut Dutch off. Dutch saw them, made a sharp left, and skidded out of control to a stop. He jumped out and looked over his shoulder. The guards who had arrested Qwan were on Dutch's ass. He tried to hop a fence, but the guards who had been entertained by Angel came out of a service entrance and were right up on him. Trapped, Dutch leaned against the fence as the security guards began going through their motions.

"Freeze," yelled the guard nearest him, his gun loaded and ready.

"Get your hands up!" yelled his partner.

Craze and Angel watched the commotion helplessly from afar. They couldn't make out who got caught and who got away, but they knew the last driver didn't make it, and Craze knew in his heart it was Dutch.

Craze plucked his blunt from the window of his Porsche. Still parked in the courthouse parking lot, he sat quietly without the radio and reflected on his best friend. *Always got to be the last man standin',* he thought to himself. He only hoped Dutch would be standing after the trial was over.

CHAPTER FIVE

♦

LOCKUP

Will you please state your name for the court, sir?"

"Kenneth Jackson," said the slim, lanky black man in the prison-provided polyester suit, the powder-blue suit that prisons gave to inmates going to court. Dutch looked at the joker on the stand. *This nigga,* he thought to himself.

Kenneth Jackson, aka Shorty, had been locked up with Dutch during an eighteen-month stint up in Annandale, New Jersey, twelve years ago, and he still looked the same. Kenneth Jackson was a petty thief, a wannabe con man on crack. He was still going in and out of prison on skid bids. He still had the nervous twitch in his right eye that became more rapid whenever he was lying. Still the same fast talker, spewing words so fast they often tripped over each other trying to come out.

"And where do you currently reside, Mr. Jackson?" asked Jacobs.

"In a halfway house off of Broad Street."

I wonder what case he got that his testimony gonna get 'em off of, thought Dutch as Jacobs got under way with his questioning.

Dutch hardly knew the man, merely saw him from time to time. Kenneth Jackson was forever on his way to jail or coming home from one. They never spoke to each other in their infrequent meetings when Dutch would be ridin' by or Shorty would be walking through a spot. However, each would always acknowledge the other's presence.

"And do you know Bernard James?"

"Of course I do—who don't? He's sitting right over there," Shorty said as he pointed his index finger at Dutch like he was viewing a police lineup.

Listen to this muhfucker, thought Dutch as he sat with his finger against his temple thinking back to how he first met that nigga.

Dutch had just been through the prison reception unit in Yardsville. He could see the sterile yellow walls and cold, metallic tile as if it was yesterday. Qwan, Dutch, and about eighteen other guys varying in age and crimes along with time, were all lined up in front of a thick yellow line drawn on the floor. No one spoke, but Dutch could tell who was scared and who wasn't just by their demeanor.

Qwan stood three heads down from Dutch, who glanced down at him as Qwan winked back. Dutch knew that out of everyone in his clique, Qwan wasn't cut out for incarceration, and he was worried about him. He hoped that wherever he was transferred, Qwan would be with him.

A sliding door clanked open and a corrections officer stepped through it. He had to weigh in at three-something and wasn't more than five foot four.

"All right! How you came into this world is how you're leaving it too. Strip!"

Many of those in the lineup had been through this ritual many times, but Dutch was one of the ones who had not. New to the bullshit, he began to undress, a little too slowly for the large CO who spotted him. The corrections officer came thundering toward him.

"You!" the CO said as he got close up in Dutch's face, so close Dutch could smell the man's breakfast on his breath. "Didn't you hear what the fuck I said? You deaf or is you just retarded?"

Dutch's whole being trembled in rage, but his composure remained unaffected. He merely continued to slowly unbutton his shirt.

"Listen here, you little black bastard, once you step inside these here walls you belong to *me*! You ain't shit, wasn't shit, and ain't gonna be shit! When I tell you to strip, motherfucker, I mean strip, not no goddamn striptease!" the CO shouted in Dutch's face.

Qwan glanced over nervously as he stood asshole naked in line with all the others who were naked or about to be, all except for Dutch. He imagined standing there eye to eye, toe to toe, with the corrections officer, then beating the motherfucker, dropping him to the ground and stomping him until the man lay lifeless. Instead, he just smiled.

"Yes, sir . . . you're the boss," Dutch spoke as the rest of his clothes dropped to the floor.

The young men were then outfitted in prison clothes, handcuffed, and shackled, ready to be shipped to the various places they would do their sentences.

The transfer buses were loaded up, but Dutch and Qwan were to head in two different directions. Dutch was to go to Mountainview and Qwan would be going to Jamesburg, known to everyone as "gladiator camp." Dutch watched in silence as Qwan boarded the bus. Qwan never looked back, and once Dutch saw that he was seated, he boarded his own bus.

Mountainview looked like a big farm surrounded by trees and distant mountains. He was definitely a long way from Newark. The camp was arranged in cottages, about ten in all. Dutch was assigned to Cottage 3. When he entered, he saw guys sitting in the day room watching TV and playing cards. He noticed a few familiar faces, but he didn't acknowledge them. He wasn't trying to be too friendly too quickly. That could be seen as meaning that he was scared or looking for protection, and since Dutch was neither, he approached no one. Someone did approach him though— Kenneth Jackson, aka Shorty.

"Now, when did you first meet Bernard James?" inquired Jacobs.

"Well, I had read about him in the paper, about how he tried to hit the port and all, but I didn't know him until he came to Mountainview."

"And can you describe him for us?"

"Well, from jump, Dutch came in like he had something to prove, you know, like he had a shoulder on his chip, I mean a chip on his shoulder. Matter of fact, he wasn't in the cottage five minutes and he was already fightin'."

Shorty had been playing cards waiting for Dutch to come through the cottage door. He found out Dutch was assigned to his cottage, and Shorty was the self-appointed cottage welcoming committee, always trying to find fear in the new jacks so he could con them. He looked at Dutch, but there was no fear of anything there. So Shorty came with a friendly face instead of a bunch of slick talk.

"Hey, ain't you Bernard James?" asked Shorty.

Dutch looked at him, never saying a word, then looked away.

"Yeah, yeah, I thought I knew you. Yeah, you use to steal cars with my man Nu Nu from down Bergen," said Shorty, his conniving mind working overtime.

Dutch looked back at the nigga. *Who the fuck is Nu Nu?* thought Dutch, knowing he didn't know any Nu Nu.

Shorty realized that approach wasn't working and tried another.

"Yo, yo y'all, this that kid who tried to rob the port, yo. His name is Bernard, yo. The nigga got heart," said Shorty, throwing Dutch to the wolves, so to speak.

"Fuck a Bernard, nigga name don't ring bells here! Fuck him and the port!" somebody hollered back.

Snickers and furtive glances were thrown at Dutch as he began making his way to the disrespectful voice belonging to a young cat a little older than him. When the cat saw Dutch coming, he stood right up and began to say something but never got it out of his mouth. Dutch caught that nigga with lightning-fast speed. He hit him with a combination that sat him back in his chair. The dude's friends spread out as the guy sprang quickly to his feet and threw up his hands.

"Oh, you nice wit' yo' shit, huh? But, ain't shit sweet here, nigga," the guy proclaimed as he slid into the boxing style known as the Brooklyn 52. He glided from side to side, bringing his hands up and around, trying to conceal his blows. He threw two blows. Dutch ducked one but was somewhat dazed by the second. The cat tried to follow up with a right hook that Dutch sidestepped as he hit back with two hard jabs of his own, catching his opponent in the mouth and eye, drawing first blood.

The fight was the center of attraction. With adrenaline pumping, niggas were standing on top of chairs and tables, screaming and hollering.

"Get yo' weight up, Duke," screamed one guy.

"Knock that muhfucker out," hollered another.

"Little man got heart," spoke another in the crowd, respecting Dutch's gangster.

They fought a bloody draw. Dutch was more bloodied than his opponent, but the point was made. Newjack or no newjack, Dutch would represent and represent to the fullest. He was brought back to the present by the sound of Shorty's voice as it got louder.

"Then bam! Dutch hit the dude in the mouth and the fight broke out. That was how Dutch came through the door."

"So, Bernard James came into the prison a violent person, is that correct?"

"I . . . mean, he wasn't no killer or nothing, but he definitely made his presence known and I respected that."

No, you didn't. You didn't respect that shit. Nigga, you feared it. After the fight, Dutch knew who was responsible for it— Shorty. *But you ain't sittin' up there telling these crackers that you started the shit.*

That's just how Shorty was, though, the type of cat who instigated fights but rarely fought one. Originally from Prince Street, one of the most notorious areas in Newark, his people's names rang bells and he lived off of their rep. Shorty was so well connected in the prison's black market it didn't make sense. Dutch learned he was a valuable liaison between the inmates and the many corrections officers who flooded the prison with drugs. However, he also knew that guys like Shorty were bad business, so he kept him at arm's length, close enough to reach, but distant enough to keep him in his place.

"Do you know of any gang activity at Mountainview?" asked Jacobs.

"Yeah, everybody in a gang, if that's what you wanna call it. Dudes just really clique up, I mean, get together on a county-versus-county or city-versus-city basis, sometimes a street-versus-street basis. It all depends on where you at to determine who you wit'."

Jacobs barely understood what Shorty had just said, but he had managed to establish that there were gangs, so he could establish Dutch's involvement in them.

"Now, I ask you, do you know if Mr. James was involved in any gang?"

"I'm sayin', everybody was 'cause really, you had to be. So, yeah, everybody was, especially Dutch," Shorty emphasized.

"Especially?"

"Dutch practically ran Mountainview, and if Newark was involved, he was on the front line. If any moves was made, Dutch didn't make 'em, he had 'em made. He was the man, bottom line."

Dutch chuckled to himself. *This nigga is ridiculous. Why is he always exaggerating?* Truth was, Dutch didn't run any-thing, let alone some kind of gang. He did run with those cats who were recognized and well-respected, but it had nothing to do with Newark. There were plenty of smooth dudes in the game who liked Dutch's style. Real recognized real, that's all it was. And he didn't run with a gang. Sure, he had earned a little rep for his hands and dudes knew how he got down. But in truth, Dutch was respected for his mind.

Nobody knew how, but Dutch ended up with a job in the library, a job he had actually wanted for some time. Most cats didn't think the wild young nigga even knew how to read, let alone want to. His choice of literature ran to Sun Tzu's *The Art of War*, Machiavelli's *The Prince*, or George Jackson's *Blood in My Eye*—and then he'd mash a nigga's face over a card game. His moods alternated, and he was unpredictable. No one trusted him except those who didn't trust themselves and therefore understood him. Only the most incorrigible and unredeemable could see the potential in Dutch. He had been raised in the streets and perfected in prison.

Within a year of Dutch's being locked down, niggas had come through with stories from the streets about who was getting it and how. The players in the drug game were getting younger and younger. Before, the old heads were on top and in control. But, gradually, they retired, went legit, got locked up, or died, leaving the streets wide open for thirsty up-and-comers.

Skeet and Phil, Kurt from Prince Street, and the Wright brothers were all making names for themselves throughout Newark. But of all of them, one name stood out the loudest, the clearest, and the deadliest—Kazami. No one knew him, either. He had just popped out of nowhere and emerged on Springfield Avenue around the time Dutch had fallen.

Within a year, he had completely taken over Newark's heroin trade. Then he gradually added Elizabeth, East Orange, Linden, and most of Jersey City. Many people thought Kazami was Haitian, but he was really Nigerian and brought a team with him that was used to guerilla warfare in the jungles of Africa, so the urban jungle was no challenge.

Murder and intimidation propelled Kazami to the top and there he stood alone, virtually unchallenged until Frank Sorbonno, aka Frankie Bonno, had moved up in the ranks of the Cerone crime family and wanted to control the city's drug trade. Frank had two hits carried out on Kazami, but missed both times, which only added to Kazami's street reputation, making him legendary.

Dutch had already heard of Kazami from Angel, who had started nickel and dimin' for one of Kazami's workers on Dayton Street. Of the whole clique, Angel was the only one who wrote to Dutch on a consistent basis. Roc, who also worked for one of Kazami's street teams, sent money from time to time, but it was Angel who kept him in the know.

She told him about everything. Shock had died in a motorcycle accident. That was the first time Dutch had cried for someone in his life. She also wrote and told him Zoom was home and he was running around sticking everything up with the Zoo Crew. Years later, they too would become legends in Newark. She also wrote telling him about her first sexual experience with a woman. Dutch already knew she was dyke material, so he wasn't at all surprised.

Craze, his main man, almost never wrote unless Angel caught him, sat him down, and made him, which was seldom. It wasn't that Craze wouldn't write. It was that he couldn't and he was ashamed. Dutch understood when he finally did get a letter from Craze and it was in the hand-writing of a child. Dutch couldn't read it to answer back, so he didn't.

Qwan wrote him a lot. He was over there in "gladia-tor camp" holding it down with the tack heads over there. Qwan always went to church, but never hesitated when he perceived someone as disrespecting him. He talked about God in every letter, but Dutch wasn't concerned with that. He was just glad Qwan was all right.

Of everyone in Dutch's young life, the one he expected to write him the most, his mother, never wrote at all. When he was in the county, Dutch wrote her several times but she never wrote back. And right after he got locked up, her phone was disconnected, and he couldn't call. He sent letters every week or so and greeting cards for every holiday and occasion, but his mail to his mother was returned to him marked CHANGE OF ADDRESS UN-KNOWN. Delores had moved and didn't even leave a for-warding address.

At first, it pained him, but he knew his mother loved him, so his pain changed to confusion, but never to stress. He had Angel find out where she moved to, but he never wrote her again. He figured he'd just go visit her when he got out. He only had one month left in prison. Dutch was now sixteen, and had grown a full two inches, and with the constant workouts in the gym, he was in tip-top shape.

He had learned many things in prison, things that would shape his immediate future and ultimate destiny. He stared around the cold cell in which he had spent the last eighteen months of his life. It was the last morning he would ever spend locked in a cage. He looked at the mirror and at himself. *I'm never coming back to no place like this again,* he promised himself. Then said it out loud, "I'm never coming back to prison. I'll hold court in the streets first."

Dutch walked out the front gate of Mountainview Correctional and never looked back.

CHAPTER SIX

◆

THE RETURN

Dutch's first sight on leaving prison was Craze sitting outside the fence in a stolen Honda Prelude.

"Fuck kinda shit you into? How you gonna pick me up in some stolen shit?" Dutch asked, finding his friend amusing.

"Oh, so these muhfuckers done got rehabilitation programs that work on niggas, now? Let me find the fuck out, they done got you all fucked up in the head and rehabilitated and shit," said Craze as he threw up his hands and playfully swung at Dutch, who blocked him and playfully threw one of his own.

On the long trip back to Newark, Craze filled Dutch in on everything he'd been doing during Dutch's absence.

"Ay, yo, you remember that chick, Sharonda? She used to live in my building? Word life, money, I gutted that bitch out!" Craze bragged as he blew a ring with his cigarette smoke.

"Nigga, please! Ain't no way you bagged that bu-gee bitch. You? Aw, hell no," Dutch replied.

"Yo, that's my word. Shortie on my dick, callin' me every

five minutes and shit, talkin' 'bout when we gonna go back to Pebbles Beach so she can suck me off," said Craze, laughing along with Dutch. Pebbles Beach was slang for the rooftop of any project apartment building.

"Let me find out, nigga. You musta' started stickin' niggas or something. Ain't no way you gonna tell me she just fuckin' you on the strength."

"Naw, yo, I been swingin' with that cat Sugar Ray from time to time and you know how Ray get down. I ain't gonna front, he been schoolin' a nigga on the broads," Craze admitted.

Dutch knew Sugar Ray was a wannabe pimp. Ray was a top player in Newark, specializing in women. And while he wasn't a real pimp in the true sense of the word, he tried his damndest to live the life of one.

"Angel said the chop shop connect got popped. Y'all ever find another one?" asked Dutch.

"Naw, you know how niggas is about connects."

"Then why you ain't start clockin' wit' Angel? She said she tried to put you on but you ain't want to. The fuck up wit' you, nigga? You and Scotty hangin' out again?" Dutch questioned, half joking, half serious.

"Fuck you, nigga. I ain't smokin' no crack." Then he turned up the radio playing Colonel Abrams's "Music Is the Answer."

"So, what is you doin'?" asked Dutch, turning the volume back down.

"Yo, I'm sayin', shit just ain't been right. It's like I been stuck, you know. You know I've known you forever and it's always been me and you. You know what I'm sayin'? Roc and Zoom my niggas and Shock, God bless the dead. Angel, she like my lil' sister. But, wit' out you . . ." Craze completed his sentence by shaking his head, not knowing how to express what he had been feeling for the past year and a half since Dutch had been gone.

Dutch understood. Craze needed to say no more.

"But, now . . . since you back, I know shit gonna be all right. Word. I know it," he said, his words expressing nothing but love for Dutch.

When they reached Newark, the streets themselves seemed to welcome Dutch home with the sounds of a hundred booming systems, children laughing, and people crowding the streets, and the urban smells mingling in Dutch's nostrils. Young women ornamented the city blocks like jewels and became the twinkle in his eyes. Dutch felt invigorated, renewed, free.

They rode up Elizabeth Avenue and made a right onto Pomona. Pomona Gardens was on the corner where Craze pulled over.

"Why she move here?" Craze asked.

Dutch didn't know, and he didn't answer. He just opened the door and got out of the car.

"Wait here," he said, walking away from Craze and over to the building he had been told his mother lived in. He searched the panel for Murphy, Delores's last name, but it wasn't listed. Luckily, someone was coming out and he entered the building and took the elevator to the fourth floor. He found 406, Delores's apartment, and knocked on the door. Waiting, he felt butterflies and nervousness. *Why didn't she write me back? And why'd she move over here?*

There was no answer.

He knocked again.

Something in his heart told him his mother was home. He decided to knock once more, but as he was about to, the door slowly opened and his mother stood in the doorway in her housecoat.

"Hey, Ma," he said, not knowing whether to hug her or just stand still.

She gazed at him momentarily, then spoke. "When you get home?"

"Today, just now," Dutch answered, feeling awkward standing in the hallway, seemingly barred from what should have been his home. She stepped aside, though, and pushed the door open wider to let him pass.

Dutch looked around the place. It was the same size as their apartment in Brick Towers, just more airy because it had more windows.

"So, you moved, huh?"

"Yeah," was all Delores said as she lit a Newport.

"Well, whatcha' do with all the stuff I bought you?" he asked.

"You bought?" she said as if he was crazy.

"Ma, listen, I know I messed up. And I know you probably mad at me, but . . ." His words made him think about all the visiting days his heart had yearned to hear his name called. Everybody else had someone waiting on them with open arms in the visiting room. "But, you coulda' came to see me at least once or wrote me back. I wrote you every week and you just moved on me."

"Because, you a goddamn fool and a coward, that's why." Delores glared as she blew out a gust of smoke.

Her words caught him by surprise. She had never cursed

him. It didn't anger him or add to the pain he already felt, but he was shocked.

"That's right, you heard me. Yous'a goddamn fool and you damn right I was mad, not at what you did, at what you didn't do. You let them muhfuckers lock you up like a damn dog?" she said with her voice a little higher. "And then you expect me to write you?" she asked again with that crazy look she'd fix her face with. "Nigga, you must be crazy, the words I had for you. Shit, better I didn't write," she said, crushing her cigarette in the ashtray.

Dutch stood quiet in the middle of the floor, head bowed. She was right; he had let them lock him up. He thought back to the night at the port, how they surrounded him with guns drawn. He gave in without a fight. Animals fight back when they're cornered, they fight to the death, but he had given up without a fight.

"You let them take you from me and you didn't do a damn thing about it. So, you damned right I left all that shit you bought me right where it was to rot, left it. All that bullshit you traded your freedom for, you expected me to keep it?" she screamed at him. He felt nervous, wondering if she would hit him. She was so emotional, yet her insanity was crystal clear to him. His mother's eighteen-month silence now spoke volumes. Every visiting day, every letter unanswered, even the unannounced change of residence said to him, *Nigga, be a man.* All that shit he had wasn't worth the time he had spent locked in a cage.

"I ain't goin' back," he said, repeating what he'd told himself earlier that day in the prison cell.

"Nigga, you goddamn right you not, 'cause I'll kill you

myself before I let you. You hear me?" she screamed. "I'll kill you myself!"

Her voice was cracking as tears rolled down her face in torrents. She had emptied her heart of the bitterness and it now lay unprotected from her emotions. Dutch felt the pain and hurt released by her words. He reached and tried to embrace her, but she shoved his hands away.

"Get off of me! Don't hug me!" she hollered at him and twirled around so he couldn't hold her. "Nigga, go on out there and take back what them people took from you!" she yelled.

Dutch had never seen his mother like this. She was always strong-willed, but she now sounded like a gang leader. He didn't know about his father and how the years without his father had worn on her. Delores had sacrificed her heart to set that man free so long ago, and for Dutch to go out and give his life away to those people was, to her, the ultimate betrayal. For everything their union represented, for all her heart's pain and for all the years of loneliness and sacrifice, she had Dutch to compensate. But she wouldn't let him disappoint her again. He turned to walk out the door.

"Bernard!" his mother called out to him.

He turned to face her, ready and willing to do anything for her.

"I just wanted to say the name," she said, turning from him.

Dutch walked out, closing the door behind him.

Craze turned the Prelude onto Dayton Street, and they saw Angel yelling at a cop car that was pulling off. She was screaming curses in Spanish like a madwoman, waving her arms up and down.

"Usted siempre estan jodiedo con nosotro. Por que no sevan a otra la do a joder. Marditos idiota!" Angel could be heard up and down the block.

"Same ol' Angel," smirked Dutch, happy to see her again.

"Naw, she worse," said Craze, shaking his head.

"Ahhh, Poppi, you're home," she said, running to Dutch with open arms. She hugged him close. "Oh, my God, I can't believe it, I missed you so much," she said while holding him.

"What's up, baby girl? How you been?" Dutch asked as she let go.

"Man, I'm chillin', but look at you," she said, admiring the difference a year and a half had made.

"Damn, you got mad taller and you done got all diesel and shit," Angel chimed.

"You too," Dutch replied, referring to the fistful of dollars she was gripping.

"This? This ain't shit, man. Them fuckin' punk-ass police got shit hot as a firecracker on the Fourth of July round this bitch. But, what's up with you?" she asked. Angel was smiling from ear to ear. She had missed Dutch like crazy and was happy he was home. Besides, she had a surprise waiting for him.

"So, what you about to do?" she asked with a twinkle in her eye.

"Why?" inquired Dutch.

"'Cause I got a surprise for you," she said with a devilish grin.

"I hope it's some pussy," cracked Dutch as Angel playfully hit him and blushed.

"No, Poppi, it ain't no pussy. It's better than that," she retorted.

"Better than a shot after eighteen months?" asked Dutch, as if to say "no way."

"Better! Just come on," she said, grabbing his arm, leading him to Craze's car. "And you better not have told him, either," she shouted to Craze with an evil eye.

"Girl, I ain't told no body nothin'," Craze said, flagging his hand at her to be quiet as he started the car.

"So, what's up with this Kazami nigga you workin' for?" asked Dutch.

"Nothin', but the nigga's definitely strong. He gettin' it from Newark to Linden. His stamp is everywhere. Bundles don't move unless it's Wild Cherry or Tango and Cash. I got that Dark Angel 'cause that Tango and Cash shit was killin' niggas and shit. So, I changed the stamp. These niggas still runnin' around lookin' for that Tango shit. Ain't they crazy?" she asked, shaking her head, not understanding a dope fiend's logic.

Dutch silently agreed as they pulled into a large junkyard off Frelinghuysen. They all got out as Mr. Ramirez came out of the garage, wiping his hands on a dirty rag.

"*Que tal,* Angel?" he asked.

"*Que pasa? El ese de quien yo te able,*" said Angel.

"Hello, Dutch, I heard a lot about you. Good to meet you," said the older Dominican man.

"And the same," said Dutch, shaking the man's hand as Craze greeted Mr. Ramirez.

"I'm ready for it," Angel said as Mr. Ramirez went back inside the garage with the three of them close behind.

"Now, we gonna do this right, so close your eyes," Angel said as she covered Dutch's eyes and navigated him to the rear of the garage. She stopped him and removed her hands from his eyes. Dutch saw a black BMW 745il with peanut butter leather interior and gold-dipped BBS rims.

"Surprise!" yelled Angel.

Dutch just looked at the BMW, then at Angel as she jumped into his arms and kissed him on the cheek. Dutch couldn't speak. For the first time in his life, he was speechless.

"Guess where it came from?" she questioned.

"Where?" Dutch asked, barely getting the word out.

"From the port that night; it's one of the cars we stole."

"This stolen?"

"Yeah, nigga, but it's tagged," she said, smiling proudly.

"Tagged?" Dutch had never heard the term before.

"Yeah, this car got the serial numbers on it from a demolished BMW out in the junkyard. We got this, don't worry."

"How the fuck I'm suppose to register it?" asked a skeptical Dutch.

"We did that already. I took care of that, don't worry," said Mr. Ramirez, patting Dutch on the back.

"And one more thing," she said, holding up a driver's license with Dutch's picture on it, just not his name.

Dutch took the license and looked at his picture in awe. He had never expected this kind of homecoming.

"Yo, how the fuck did you . . ."

" 'Cause, nigga, I love you, man. I missed you," said Angel with tears in her eyes, so happy he was happy.

"Thank you, both y'all, man. Nobody's ever did nothing like this for me, ever," he said pulling her close and tight.

"Aww, man, this ain't nothing but a jazzed-up jack move," Craze complained as he watched the two get all sentimental.

"Shut up!" spat Angel.

"I don't know who she think she be talkin' to," grumbled Craze with aggravation.

"So, is you gonna be out today or tomorrow?" Craze asked Dutch as Mr. Ramirez held out the key. Dutch took it and walked around to the driver's side, admiring his new whip. The panther-black paint reflected from the lights in the garage. The car sparkled like it was covered in diamonds. Angel took the passenger seat as Dutch breathed in the new-leather interior smell. He backed out of the garage and Angel waved good-bye to Mr. Ramirez. He drove slowly to where Craze was parked in the Prelude.

"Yo, Duke, I gotta few things to do. I'll holla at you later, i-ight?" said Craze.

"I-ight," said Dutch.

"Welcome home," Craze said, pulling off with a smile and love for his man.

Dutch started his car and headed back around to Dayton Street with Angel riding shotgun. He pulled over on the side of the street.

"I got something else for you, too. Stay here," said Angel, climbing out of the car. Dutch watched her walk across the street as she started hollering.

"Vita! Yo, Vita! *Ven aqui!*" Angel hollered up the block.

The young Dominican girl heard her name being called and turned around to see it was Angel and began waving. Her hair was long, stretching down her back. She had on a skirt and a halter-top, revealing as much as could be revealed outside in the streets.

"Vita, this is Dutch. Dutch, this is Vita," she said, making an introduction.

"*Que pasa*, Poppi?" Vita asked as she leaned her fat ass against the frame of his BMW.

"*Te gusta?*" Angel asked her.

"*Si,*" Vita answered, giggling and smiling.

"She doesn't speak much English, but she speaks body language like a muhfucka," Angel told Dutch before turning to Vita.

"*Quiero que lo agas sentirse vien?*" said Angel, questioning Vita's capabilities to please Dutch.

Vita eyed Dutch seductively as she received Angel's orders. Dutch was erect just watching Vita standing there with her voluptuous body hanging out of her skirt and halter-top. Vita had beautifully toned legs and the perfect waist to finish her perfect frame. Dutch licked his lips and smiled, jerking his head calmly for her to get in the car with him.

"Make sure you save me some!" Angel said, walking away.

Dutch turned around and looked at Angel, wondering if she was talking to him or Vita.

It was 3:13 A.M. Dutch lay on his back with his hands behind his head, looking at the ceiling in the cheap hotel room. Vita was curled up beside him under the covers. He lay deep in thought as cool, soothing air breezed over his bare body. The sweet release of eighteen months had come and gone several times during the course of the night. And like a man with a ravishing hunger who eats until he's full, he no longer desired food.

Dutch thought of where he was and where he wanted to be. He contemplated his next move, knowing that stealing cars was a thing of the past, a past he didn't want to return to. He would always love the thrill of the chase, of stealing cars, of speeding. But the short bid he had served brought on an accelerated maturity, and he realized that the rewards were no longer worth the risks. He wanted bigger rewards, which would mean bigger risks. His mother's unusual and unexpected talk had convinced him of what he had already known.

He could never go back to prison.

He thought about an offer Angel had made to get Barrett to put him on. Dutch couldn't see it though, nickel and dimin' for somebody else. Hell no! That wasn't for Dutch, but the lines had been drawn while he was away.

Kazami had made his presence felt and feared. Then on the other side, there was Frankie Bonno. Frankie Bonno represented Fat Tony. They were the same family. To work for Kazami would be to choose the opposition, not that he felt loyal to Fat Tony. It was more than that. He knew Kazami wasn't the kind of ally he needed in this war. It was only a matter of time before Frankie Bonno made good on a hit. Dutch shook his head and got up out of bed and pulled on his pants.

He stood over Vita, looking down on the imprints her curves made under the covers, and felt himself starting to harden again, but he quickly pushed her out of his mind. He thought about his mother and what she had told him.

Go out there and take back what they took from you! She's right, he thought. He was young, black, and free, with nothing to lose, and there was nothing more dangerous than that combination.

Just then an idea hit him like a brick in the face, so hard it almost physically staggered him.

Kill Kazami! Fuckin' Frankie Bonno don't know what the fuck he's doing. Take Kazami and his blocks, Dutch thought as he sat down, thinking of the money that would be his by knocking Kazami off and taking over his turf.

CHAPTER SEVEN

◆

REVEREND TAYLOR

The State calls Reverend Eqwan Taylor, Your Honor," Jacobs announced, as proud as a peacock, staring over at Dutch.

I know you're scared now, thought Jacobs as he looked over at Dutch, hoping to catch a glimmer of fear or a slight wince of pain at the sound of one of his closest friends' being called to the stand. But, to Jacobs's dismay, Dutch maintained the same nonchalant aloofness as he had throughout the trial. *You won't be so goddamn smug after this, I betcha, you black bastard.*

Reverend Eqwan Taylor, aka Qwan, slowly made his way to the stand. It had been years since he had seen Dutch, but he was still the Dutch he remembered. He was richer, but had the same attitude, the same demeanor. Qwan had left New Jersey right after the "Month of Murder," or so the newspapers had called it. It was actually Dutch's murdering spree. Truth was, Qwan was never the murderous type. He only rolled with Dutch in the beginning because he was young, bored, and liked to drive cars, fast. So he stole them. Prison was a turmoil that seemed to escalate into freedom for Qwan as Dutch's murder spree carried Dutch to the top of Newark's drug trade. It was more than Qwan could stomach, to say the least.

"Yo, Dutch, I need to talk to you," Qwan remembered saying to Dutch, as he approached the witness stand. He remembered how Dutch had looked at him; how he never said more than a few words their entire conversation.

"Dutch, man, I," he stopped, trying to find the words. "I wake sometimes at night in a sweat and tears and I can't tell the difference between the two. It's so many people dyin', too many. I keep thinkin' somebody's gonna kill me or my mother or my sister. Don't you ever think like that?" Qwan asked.

"No."

"Well, I do, man. I think about it a lot. And, yo, I couldn't live with myself if something I did caused my family pain, I mean . . ." Qwan drifted off thinking about the last murder, the last death, the blood all on him. "It ain't in me, Dutch. It ain't. I can't do it no more. If I said it was in me, I'd be frontin'."

"Ain't no future in that," Dutch said, real short.

"Naw, it ain't. So, yo . . . I'm out. I'm gonna go out to Cali and stay with my aunt, Duke."

Dutch just looked at him for a moment, and Qwan knew what Dutch was thinking. *Should I let this nigga go or should I . . .* But Dutch broke the silence by reaching into his pocket and handing Qwan a large roll of money. Qwan later counted it out to be over five thousand dollars.

"One love," Dutch said before he walked off. Qwan hadn't seen him since.

• • •

Now, look at him, up on the stand, testifying with his hand raised up in the air.

"I do," Qwan said as he took a seat on the witness stand.

He tried to avoid looking at Dutch, but it was like his eyes were magnetized by Dutch's and he couldn't help it. Dutch locked in on him for a split second, and, surprisingly, Dutch's gaze was ambivalent but welcoming. It made Qwan more nervous than he already was.

Jacobs stood up slowly and made a ceremony of putting on his glasses as he approached the witness stand.

"Sir, please state your name for the court."

"Reverend Eqwan Taylor," Qwan said as he leaned toward the microphone.

"And can you please tell us where you are currently residing?"

"In Los Angeles, California."

"And what do you do in Los Angeles, if I may ask?" Jacobs asked, as if the title "reverend" weren't obvious enough.

"I'm the reverend of the First Street Baptist Church, and I'm also the founder of an organization called Mindstate for Youth Against Drugs," Qwan proudly stated.

Jacobs inwardly smiled at the irony, while Dutch outwardly grinned at the same time.

"How long have you been in California, Reverend Taylor?"

"About ten years,"

"Where did you live prior to California?" inquired Jacobs.

"Right here, in Newark," Qwan replied.

"Were you in Newark in April of 1987?"

"Yes, I was."

"And were you in any way connected to the defendant, Bernard James?"

"Yes."

"In what way?"

"We were friends," Qwan stated, hearing himself say those words and questioning for the first time his own presence at the proceedings.

"Reverend Taylor, is it true that you and Bernard James went to prison together for grand larceny?"

"Yes."

Jacobs turned slightly to the jury, then paced the open floor of the courtroom.

"Now Reverend Taylor, for the record, you are aware that the testimony you are about to give has been granted total immunity?"

"I am aware of that," Qwan replied.

"Then, Reverend, on or about April of 1987, could you please tell the court what you and the defendant discussed?"

"We discussed killing Kazami, a local drug dealer," Qwan said hesitantly.

"Please speak up, Reverend, so the court can hear you," said Jacobs as he riffled through a file on his desk while Qwan repeated himself louder for the court.

"Reverend Taylor, could you, for the court and to the best of your ability, tell us what was said in that discussion regarding the murder of Ojiugo Kazami?" Jacobs asked, struggling with the Nigerian's name.

Qwan readjusted himself in his chair and began to tell the story that had incessantly haunted him for the last ten years. It was the story that had chased him to California and had summoned him back to relive it.

• • •

Dutch pulled up in the black BMW. Qwan recognized it and knew Angel had saved it for him from the port. Dutch had asked everybody to meet him in front of Craze's building on Sixteenth Avenue.

"Is your aunt home?" Dutch asked Craze.

"Naw, come on."

No one really knew what Dutch was up to, but all Qwan could think was that the last time Dutch had called a meeting, he ended up with a fourteen-month prison stay. Everyone was there just like before, Zoom, Roc, Angel, Craze, and Dutch. They entered Craze's aunt's apartment and everybody took seats around the living room and dining room, which occupied the same floorspace, while Dutch remained standing.

"Listen, what I'm about to put y'all up on ain't like nothin' we ever did before. So, if you not gonna be 'bout it, leave now, 'cause ain't no need for you to know nothing."

Dutch looked around the room and stopped his gaze on Qwan. It was then that Qwan first felt the urge to leave, but since no one else made any attempt to, he didn't want to be the one to look scared, even though he was.

"Before me and Qwan fell, we was together, all of us, like a family, you know what I'm sayin'? We ate together, slept together, wore each other's shit, the whole nine. But it ain't like that now. Everybody doing their own thing, which is nothing wrong with that, but you doin' it for somebody else. The way I see it, this nigga is the cat to see. His whole clique clockin' the type of ends muhfuckas only see in a lottery and anybody on the opposing team is gonna starve, bottom line. That's where we come in. We the opposing team, so it's us that's gonna starve."

"How you figure that? Me and Angel on the nigga team.

I'm on Prince, Angel on Dayton, and we got the shit sewn up," said One-eyed Roc.

"Naw, Roc, he got shit sewn up. You ain't got a damn thing. You aint' got shit and you ain't shit to that nigga. You just some young nigga pushin' his packages, sweatin' his nickel and dimes. You probably ain't never even talked to the nigga, have you?"

"Naw."

"How 'bout you?" Dutch asked Angel. She shook her head no.

"Regardless, we gettin' ours and he gettin' his. Ain't much to discuss," Roc stated.

"Roc, who you think gonna take the fall when the shit start to stink? You! The way I see it, we got two choices. Either get a job and join the choir, 'cause if we gonna play the game ain't no need in half steppin', or we bring the family back together and go all the fuck out," Dutch said with authority.

"So, what? You sayin' we cop and go for self?" asked Angel.

"Go for self! How we gonna do that? See what happened to Lil' Nicki from Seventh Avenue and Smiley from Bergen when they tried that shit? Kazami murdered them niggas and they been gettin' money," Zoom said.

"I ain't sayin' we compete with Kazami. I'm sayin' we kill Kazami," Dutch said as he looked around the room and made sure he had everyone's attention.

"Kill Kazami?" Roc exclaimed, right before he burst into laughter.

"Nigga, you been gone too long! Yo, Dutch, I love you to death. But goddamn, son, what the fuck is you on?" asked

Zoom between laughs. "Even the mob can't kill this nigga and you expect us to?" he said, slapping fives with Roc.

Dutch hated to be laughed at, but since he had expected derision and disbelief, he maintained his composure. He looked around knowing that whatever he did, Craze and Angel would be with him. Qwan would roll with the tide, but Roc controlled it. So Dutch turned his attention on Roc.

"Dig, Money, the shit sound crazy, real crazy. But, let me tell you, while you out grindin' and sweatin', duckin' 5-0 and shit, what you think that nigga's doin'?"

"Man, I don't know," said Roc, wondering where this all came from.

"I'll tell you, he spendin' your ends, fuckin' wit' bitches that won't even speak to you. Pushin' whips you can't even steal and when you get knocked, get stuck, or get killed, what is he gonna do? He's gonna get another nigga to re-place you. Now tell me that shit ain't crazy, too," Dutch said and watched as his words penetrated Roc's thinking cap.

"Zoom, me and you, we go way back, right?" Dutch asked, now turning his attention to Zoom.

"Yeah, no doubt, you my man," Zoom answered, shaking his head.

"So, out of everybody in here, you know me like I know you. So, you know I know you ain't tryin' to be no petty-ass stick-up kid vickin' niggas for coats and gold chains, seein' a grand here and a grand there. Fuck kinda shit is that?"

"Hell naw! I wanna live like live-ass niggas live, but, yo, killin' Kazami?" Zoom twisted up his face. "That muhfucka would murder us if he even thought we was thinkin' 'bout stickin' him, let alone killin' him," he finished.

"And? Shit, every time you pull out your gun, Zoom,

you make another enemy. Ain't no way you remember every face, every car, or every cat you lick, nigga. Who's to say a nigga don't catch you slippin' one day? Then what? They gonna kill you, that's what. Murder you over a petty-ass coat or hundred-dollar chain, so do it matter who kill you? Naw, nigga, it only matters what you die for. At least if we do die tryin' to kill Kazami, it's better than dyin' for a nigga coat, Zoom. Or 'cause you came short on his money, Roc," Dutch added as the room remained silent for a moment.

"But, if we do get this off, we can live like muhfuckas 'posed to live, like we always dreamed. I can see that shit, yo, taste that shit, and I can't see no muhfucka livin' the life meant for me. I'd be a goddamn coward if I did," Dutch said, speaking to his clique but remembering his mother's words to him.

Everyone studied the floor or took little looks at one another until Angel stood up.

"I don't know why y'all taking so long. Fuck is you thinkin'? Y'all a bunch of bitches or somethin'? Y'all scared of that pussy-ass nigga? Fuck, he bleed just like you!"

Dutch watched Angel check the room as everyone exchanged glances, denying that they were scared. Dutch just smiled. He knew the tide was rolling his way.

"Man, I see what you sayin', but what can we do?" Roc asked.

"No, the question is, what can't you do, Roc? That's how muhfuckas think when they hungry, ya dig?"

"Like you said, man, I'm just a runner. I don't even know where the nigga rest at," Roc admitted.

"I do," Angel announced proudly, willing and able to

aid Dutch in any way he needed. "He rest in Roselle. He used to fuck wit' this bitch named Sheryl, own a beauty parlor downtown. But, now he fuck wit' Sheryl cousin and Sheryl's hot over that shit and she stay volunteering 411 as it is."

Dutch paced the floor, stopping in front of the living room window overlooking the streets that would soon be his.

"You say he got a girl?"

"Mmm-hmm," Angel nodded.

"Then we go at her."

"What? Kidnap her or somethin'?" asked Angel. "'Cause she might be his girl and all that, but a nigga like Kazami cancel bitches like bad checks and cash in on others. So he ain't breakin' his neck for a bitch."

This was true and everyone would agree on it, but Dutch had other ideas, other plans.

"Naw, not kidnap the bitch. We get her to set him up," Dutch replied, as everyone digested what he was actually saying.

"How?" Zoom understood but wanted to hear more.

Dutch just smiled as he looked at Craze, then at Roc, and then back at Zoom, "Sugar Ray."

That fine, smooth-talking, chocolate-brown-velvet, caramel-tasting black man was something else with the women and a sure way to the girl.

"Yeah, but if Sugar Ray find out what we doin' he ain't gonna want no parts in that!" said Roc, knowing Sugar Ray's bitches bent backward for him.

"Look here, it ain't a nigga alive gonna stop me from gettin' this nigga—not her, not the mob, and damn sure not Sugar Ray. So, if he don't do it, I'll murder him and any other muhfuckas standin' between me and Kazami," Dutch said, dead serious, meaning every word.

Qwan looked into Dutch's face and there was no doubt he meant it.

Qwan retold the story of that first meeting in great detail, almost word for word, as he sat on the witness stand. It was easy for him, as he had played that scene out over and over in his mind for a long time, berating himself and regretting that he didn't get up and leave when he had the chance. He also questioned why no one else got up and left that day. But they were seventeen-year-old kids with no foreseeable future until Dutch gave them one. The have-nots would have and if they didn't, then they'd die trying. But God had other plans for Qwan, and he knew that as he sat very still in the witness stand thinking of past demons.

"Reverend Taylor! Reverend Taylor, are you okay?" asked Jacobs. He needed Qwan's full attention and focus. The reverend did not realize just what his testimony had done for his case, but Jacobs was acutely aware.

"I'm okay, yes . . . yes . . . I'm fine," Qwan said, coming back to the reality of the courtroom in which he was sitting, where he was telling his deepest secrets, secrets he had harbored all his adult life.

"I realize this must be difficult for you to relive, Reverend Taylor. Should you like, we could take a short recess?"

"Well . . . If it isn't too much to ask, I think I need a moment," Qwan said weakly, which, unsurprisingly, annoyed Jacobs. His offer was one of courtesy, not one he expected to be accepted. *What the fuck,* he sighed to himself before turning to the judge.

"Your Honor, I ask for a short recess on behalf of my witness."

"This court stands for a fifteen-minute recess on behalf of the reverend," Judge Whitaker said, banging his gavel.

"Thank you, Your Honor," replied Jacobs, not grateful at all.

Qwan, on the other hand, was relieved. He needed a cigarette, and he badly needed to get out of that room. He had felt Dutch's eyes on him throughout his testimony and it felt good to be away from him.

As soon as he began to walk out of the courtroom, he caught Dutch smiling at him. And for the life of him, he knew he'd never be free.

Nigga, them demons you carrying around wit' you ain't goin' nowhere! They gonna be there for the rest of your life. You think your testimony gonna change something in this life, nigga, 'cause you confessed something for who, for who, them crackers. Naw, that's all you did. Think you doing something for yourself, nigga you ain't! Qwan heard just what Dutch's smile meant.

Outside, Qwan was puffing on his Newport, thinking incessantly, trying to calm down. He remembered how he'd first met Dutch, how they got locked up together. Man, it was all Dutch's idea, and he ended up in Jacksonville fighting a bunch of demons from Newark.

He lit another Newport from his first and thought back to the day they went to see Sugar Ray.

"Man, you little niggas done went crazy," Sugar Ray said in his slow, smooth, southern drawl.

Qwan, Dutch, and Craze had gone to see Sugar Ray at his favorite hangout, a poolroom in Elizabeth on St. George's Avenue.

Sugar Ray wasn't only a ladies' man, he was also an expert pool hustler who would take young rich white boys hanging out at the poolroom for hundreds of dollars at a time.

"How the fuck you think of some shit like that? Why would you think of some shit like that?" Ray drawled as he chalked up his cue stick and eyed the next shot.

"Anybody could get it," said Dutch.

"Yeah," Ray answered back, banking the nine ball in the side pocket, then looking up at Dutch. "That shit goes both ways." Then he walked around the table to analyze his next shot. "Look here, youngun, you know the man you talkin' 'bout hittin' done had two hits put on him? By the mob at that, and guess what? They missed both times. So what the hell makes you think some lil' niggas like y'all gon' get this muhfucka?"

" 'Cause they hittin' at him the wrong way. That's why we need you," Dutch explained as Sugar Ray sat back, lit a Newport, and listened. "That's why we need you, Sugar Ray. His broad is the weak link."

"They always are," chuckled Ray.

"So I figure if anybody could bag this chick, it'd be you. Shit, the mob might miss, but everybody knows Sugar Ray don't!" Dutch said, smiling and stroking Ray's ego. Ray knew he was being stroked too, but his vanity was too stimulated not to bite.

"Ray don't never miss no ho he go after, 'cause he don't go after every ho," Ray stated, speaking about himself in the third person.

Dutch took out two thousand dollars and handed it to Ray, whose eyes lit up like the tip of his cigarette every time he inhaled. He smoked out of the side of his mouth, holding the cigarette with his lips as he thumbed through the wad of money.

"That's just a little something to think about, to show you we dead-ass. And even if you swing on the girl and miss, my word, the BM's yours," Dutch promised.

"The BMW?" Ray's interest was definitely perking up. Ray sat back, rubbing his chin, and inspected the young man in front of him. *Who is this nigga?* he thought to himself. He knew Craze and liked the little dude, and Craze had told him a lot about Dutch while he was locked up. He knew the cat had heart trying the port. *But this nigga is crazy, trying to knock that nigga, Kazami, and I know he not really gonna bet his BMW, is he?*

Kazami was the biggest heroin dealer in North Jersey. So far, he was untouchable. Ask the mob. *What the hell, I'll just tell the lil' nigga I missed and cop the Beemer. If he try to get funny, I'll whoop his lil' ass.*

"Okay," Ray finally stated. "Show Ray this bitch, but I'ma tell you lil' niggas something 'bout baggin' broads, especially the kind that fuck wit' niggas like Kazami. See, that nigga can give a bitch everything she want, except that understanding, which niggas like him ain't got time to provide. That's where Sugar Ray come in at, lil' man. I'm the shelter in a bitch storm. But see, Sugar Ray need a storm," said Sugar Ray, continuing to talk about himself in the third person.

"A storm?" asked Dutch.

Yeah, muhfucka, you in over your head. Maybe, I won't even have to crack on this bitch. I'll just talk this nigga out his head.

"Yeah, a storm. Some emotional shit that Kazami can't buy his way out of. A storm."

"Like what?" Craze asked, not understanding.

"I don't know, youngun, shit," said Ray, taking a long drag on yet another Newport. "Go kill the bitch daddy or somethin'." Ray chuckled, blowing out smoke, knowing these young asses couldn't pee straight, let alone be crazy enough to do something like what he had just suggested. He started laughing a little harder.

Dutch just smiled at him as if they were sharing the joy.

"We'll call you," he said before turning and walking away. Craze shook Ray's hand, then he and Qwan rolled out behind Dutch.

"Yeah, lil' man, you do that," he said, stuffing the two grand Dutch had handed him into his pocket.

Back on the stand, Qwan felt a little more relaxed from his cigarette break until Jacobs began questioning him about the story of Mr. and Mrs. Smith.

"So, you say that Sugar Ray suggested it, even though he wasn't serious about you doing it?"

"Yes, Dutch knew Ray wasn't taking him serious, so he did it to show Ray and us that he was prepared to do anything to get Kazami."

"Can you tell us about the murder of Mr. Smith?"

Dutch listened as Qwan began to tell his story, but Dutch was there and knew what Qwan was about to say. He remembered how he felt killing Mr. Smith. That death served as a message not only to Kazami, but to Ray and his clique as well. But the stronger message he sent was that he proved to everyone that he could do anything to get what he wanted . . .

Anything.

The Smith family lived in Paterson, New Jersey, a small town compared to Newark, but with the same kind of people. The poor and working class rubbed elbows in the daily struggle for survival. But compared to Newark, Paterson was a suburb.

Simone came from a respectable home. Her mother was a schoolteacher and her father was a mechanic who owned his own garage. Angel had found out the address, through one of Sheryl's customers at the hair salon.

Dutch, Craze, and Qwan drove up to the house and parked down the block. The street was dark and deserted, in a neighborhood where nightfall represented dinnertime and quality family time before bedtime. No one expected that the serenity of the street would be shattered the way it was on that night. Afterward it would never be the same.

Craze carried a nine-millimeter handgun, the only gun among them. They had driven down to Paterson in silence, Craze in anticipation, Dutch in deep thought, and Qwan in a state of suspended disbelief. *I'm not doing this. As soon as the car stops, I'm jumping out. Fuck! I can't kill this girl's father, I can't.*

Qwan couldn't stomach the thought. The man was innocent, had never done anything to them. Murdering Kazami was different. Qwan wasn't for that either, but he was from the streets. If his number came up, nobody cried foul. But, Dutch wasn't playing fair. *I wonder what he will do if I just*

tell him I don't want to go. What if he thinks I'll go to the police?
I better not say nothing.

Qwan didn't either; he just rode into the night praying
for a miracle that would never come. He was too scared to
speak—he didn't know how. When they were separated and
they went to their separate jails, Qwan lost time with Dutch
and no longer knew him or trusted him.

Dutch got out of the car first. He was carrying a plate of
chicken wrapped in aluminum foil. It was the decoy Dutch
said would get them in the door. Craze and Qwan stood out
of sight on both sides of the front door while Dutch rang the
doorbell.

No one came.

Qwan hoped and prayed no one would answer. *Be asleep,*
God let them be asleep or not here. But the sound of footsteps on
the stairs bottomed out his heart of all hope.

"Who is it?" Mrs. Smith asked, pushing the door curtain
aside to peer out of the glass design.

"Hi, Mrs. Smith? I'm the friend Simone told you about. She
said you'd be expecting me." Dutch spoke like a choirboy.

"No," Mrs. Smith's face contorted in confusion, "I'm not
expecting anybody."

"I swear that Simone said she'd call you and tell you we'd
be stopping by. My grandmother's birthday is today and we
were visiting. She asked if I'd drop you some chicken by," he
said, holding up the plate. "She musta forgot to call you."

"Well, that girl is always surprising me with things, God
bless her heart. You say it's fried chicken, huh?" she asked as
she unlocked the door. She opened the door and Dutch held
out the tray and smiled.

"Surprise."

Before Mrs. Smith could thank him, Qwan and Craze came around the door as Craze stuck a gun in Mrs. Smith's face and shoved her against the wall. Dutch put on his gloves and proceeded into the living room, where Craze had Mrs. Smith in a chokehold with the gun to her head and where her husband stood in the middle of the room.

"Who the hell are you?" asked Mr. Smith, all 235 pounds of him raging, his bull kept at bay by the gun to his wife's head.

"I'm here for Simone, but since she's not here, one of you will do."

The large man didn't understand what Dutch was talking about. He didn't catch the true gravity behind the words. All he knew was that three hoodlums had barged into his home and were holding his wife at gunpoint. Every muscle in his body flexed, the vein that ran down from his forehead to his neck pulsated with rage, but he remained as still as a stone.

"Take what the hell you want and get the hell out of my house!" Mr. Smith bellowed.

"I intend to, but before I do, I want you to know about your daughter, Simone."

"What about my daughter? What have you done to her?"

"It's not what I did to Simone, it's what I'm going to do to you," Dutch said as he walked over to Mrs. Smith, as Craze pushed her into the wall and took aim.

Mr. Smith never had a chance to react.

Craze squeezed the trigger three times, hitting the man in the chest. Mr. Smith fell to the floor.

"No! No! Harris, no!" screamed Mrs. Smith at the top

of her lungs for her husband's life. Tears fell as she screamed
again, "No! God no!"

Dutch approached her with a large hunting knife and put
it to her throat.

"You hear me? Look at me!" Dutch ordered.

Mrs. Smith's heart was pounding fast; she was scared. As
she looked down on her husband's bleeding body, she saw
Craze fire two more bullets into the man's head, leaving him
lifeless.

Dutch grabbed her by the arm and the back of the neck,
forcing her to look first at him and then at her husband's
lifeless, murdered body.

"You see that? You see it? You tell your daughter this is
all her fault! He fuckin' wit' the right one now and you next
if we gotta come back! You hear me? Now you tell Kazami
that!"

It was too much for the fragile woman of forty-eight to
bear, and she fainted in Dutch's arms. He let her drop to the
floor.

The entire courtroom was silent as Qwan finished his
story. He dropped his head, teary-eyed on the stand. "All he
said was, 'Let's go,'" he mumbled almost in a whisper. Many
of the jury members were in tears; the rest eyed Dutch with
murder in their eyes. Even Jacobs was amazed at the level of
savage butchery of which Dutch was capable.

Jacobs wanted to milk Qwan's testimony for all it was
worth, but he couldn't muster up the energy to continue.
His own voice cracked as he spoke.

"No, no more questions, Your Honor," he said as he
headed back to the prosecutors' table.

"Your witness, defense," ordered Judge Whitaker.

Michael Glass slowly began to rise from his chair when Dutch grabbed his hand. Glass looked at him and Dutch shook his head no.

"What's the problem?" Glass asked.

"Let him go," Dutch answered, never taking his eyes off Qwan.

"Let him what?" Glass whispered back in shock, his face torn up. "Are you crazy? On his testimony alone the jury is ready to fry you! Let him go? Look at that jury over there. They want your blood! Now!"

Dutch slowly turned to Glass and simply repeated, "Let . . . him . . . go," keeping eye contact with Glass to let him know how serious he was.

"Defense, it's your witness," the judge repeated.

"Just a minute, Your Honor," Glass said, again looking at Dutch, who was looking at Qwan's bowed head.

"The defense has no questions, Your Honor."

The courtroom burst into astonished chitter-chatter, which ran wild through the room as the judge called for silence with his gavel.

"Order, I say. Order in the court!"

Jacobs looked at Glass in amazement. Glass simply shrugged his shoulders. At that moment, Glass knew Dutch was crazy. He had heard that he was insane, but not crazy enough to hang himself. *If he won't let me do my job, no one can blame me in the end,* he thought to himself.

"Reverend Taylor, you may step down," the judge informed Qwan.

Dutch watched the man he'd known and loved for so long slowly get down off the witness stand. He couldn't

help but think of Craze and how he predicted this day
would come.

"I told you that nigga not built for this shit, son," Craze
said after Dutch told him Qwan was leaving for California.

"He said he scared something is going to happen to his
family," Dutch said, shrugging his shoulders as if there was
nothing he could do.

"Man, that nigga Qwan know too much, way too much,"
said Craze, his eyes telling Dutch what had to be done. "Let
me take care of it, Dutch. I know you a little personal with
the nigga and shit, but fuck that. You can't let that nigga
walk no where."

"What's he going to do? Nothing but go out to California and what, become a preacher or some shit. Man, leave
that nigga alone. Let him go. If that's what he wants to do,"
said Dutch, never thinking that Qwan would really become
a preacher. Not to mention come back one day and testify
against him. Craze meanwhile had it all figured out and
was prepared to kill Qwan out in California, but Dutch
refused.

Now he had spilled his guts to the twelve people who
held Dutch's life in their hands, and again he refused, because he understood.

Dutch knew why Qwan had gone to California. He understood why he became a man of God. He pictured Qwan
preaching to lost souls and could imagine him doing a fine
job working with the youths. He knew that, for Qwan, it
wasn't a witness stand, and he also knew Qwan had no mali-
cious intent toward him.

To Qwan, the stand was a confessional. After all these years, he finally had a chance to exonerate himself, in his own eyes, and Dutch understood. When all was said and done, Dutch understood.

Qwan passed without looking in Dutch's direction and Dutch didn't look in his. And even though no words or glances were exchanged, there was relief in Qwan's passing . . .

Now, he would finally be free.

"Is the state ready to call its next witness?"

CHAPTER EIGHT

◆

THE SETUP

Craze sat in his Porsche, almost falling asleep. The trial was coming to an end and the time was drawing near. So much had been done, so much to do. *I can't believe Qwan testified like that.* Craze had told Dutch he would chirp like a bird if ever under pressure, but Dutch never listened. *And there he was chirpin', just like I said he would be,* Craze thought to himself as he thought back to where Qwan had left off.

While they carried Mr. Smith's body out on a covered stretcher, they brought Mrs. Smith out in a straitjacket. She spent the next seven months in Bellevue Hospital.

Sugar Ray was shocked to learn that his advice had been followed so precisely and scared to know these young wolves were definitely serious. But when Dutch and Craze had driven Ray to Bellevue Hospital to show him Simone, he knew that the plan could actually work. They sat across the street from Bellevue and watched as Simone came out of the hospital to where Kazami was waiting. Simone's mother had refused to see her, blaming the death of her father on her wild lifestyle. Simone came out in tears. When Kazami and his two henchmen approached her to show her the waiting car, she pushed away from him, screaming in his face, then ran for the subway. Kazami jogged after her, calling her name.

After that, Simone was putty in Ray's expert hands. It took some time, but Craze remembered the day when Sugar Ray called and said, "It's done."

Craze told Dutch and they headed over to Sugar Ray's apartment. When they arrived, Sugar Ray opened the door wearing a red silk robe and red silk slippers and smoking a Newport.

"Come on in, lil' niggas, come on in. Don't forget to take yo' shoes off 'cause Sugar Ray got that precious shit up in here," he said as he stepped aside, allowing them to pass.

Craze and Dutch kicked their shoes off at the door and followed Ray down the hall and into the living room. The thick white carpet felt like a cloud under their feet. A lengthy fish tank lined one wall of the living room and the other wall was covered with a wall unit. Teddy Pendergrass was playing in the background as Sugar Ray sat down in a green leather recliner and reclined. Craze and Dutch sat cattycorner to him.

"Yeah, lil' nigga, the bitches keep Sugar Ray living real good," he said as he saw them admiring his apartment.

"You called?" Dutch asked.

"Yeah, yeah, youngun, I called," Sugar Ray drawled out in an extra-syrupy countrified voice.

He had the floor and intended to keep them on his time. "You know, youngun, you'sa treacherous muhfucka, you know that," Ray told Dutch as he rubbed his chin. "I'ma be honest wit' you. I ain't think y'all lil' niggas would pull this shit off for real, but when I read how you left that bitch father . . ." Ray shook his head in admiration. "I knew right then I was fuckin' wit' some thoroughbred-type lil' niggas."

Ray paused to give Dutch a chance to respond, but Dutch sat quietly, so Ray continued.

"So, who did the ol' man, huh? You?" Ray asked, referring to Dutch.

"Whut you writin', a book?" Dutch responded, and Ray chuckled.

"Naw, youngun, nothin' like that. I just think shouldn't be no secrets, 'tween partnas, you know what I'm sayin'?"

Dutch knew exactly what he was implying: *partners.*

Ray leaned forward in his chair and put his feet on the floor.

"That sound 'bout right, don't it? 'Cause, you know, the way I see it is, no doubt, you did the heavy shit, 'cause you know, Ray ain't no killer, but ahhh . . . you did come to me, am I right?"

Dutch just looked at Ray with a curious little smile that Ray couldn't figure out, but he was too smooth to show the ruffle in his feathers.

"Of course you did, 'cause you had a bitch to crack and you knew Sugar Ray crack five bitches like five knuckles, then ball my fist, right? So, it's only right for a fifty-fifty job, we do a fifty-fifty split."

Dutch nodded as he listened, then spoke.

"I see what you sayin'. Like you said, we did call you. So, fifty-fifty is cool, but on one condition."

Ray wasn't prepared for a proposition. He had figured on doing all the proposing. After all, he had the trump card, but he asked anyway.

"Condition?"

"You come with us, 'cause I mean, we could lick then come back and tell you anything and if you feel like you been shitted on we might ruin this beautiful partnership," Dutch explained.

Sugar Ray dragged on his cigarette, then crushed it in the ashtray. He hadn't thought about being there personally, but then again, he had to ensure his own interest.

"I ain't got no problem with that," Ray answered and shook Dutch's hand.

"So, can we get down to business now?"

"The bitch is done for. It took a minute 'cause Ray knew what was on the line, so I made sure the shit was laid real thick, but ahhh," he held out his jeweled hand and pointed to a large gold nugget ring that was covered in diamonds. "This used to be Kazami's . . . just like his bitch. Plus, I got two one-way tickets to Georgia in the bedroom. She think we gonna go together after the shit go down. But Ray rolls alone. Besides, if Kazami can't trust the ho, how I'm 'posed to? So, how 'bout makin' sure Simone take the trip wit' Kazami and not wit' me?" Ray asked, hoping it wasn't too much to ask for.

Dutch already intended on that, so he nodded in agreement.

"Good. Now, the nigga don't keep no real paper in the crib, maybe a couple hundred thousand. But as for his real money, she don't know. Nigga sprung, but he damn sure ain't a fool. As for the safehouses, there's two, one in Newark and one in Elizabeth."

"I already got that covered," Dutch informed him. He had two teams ready to move in on the safehouses filled with heroin.

"Now, he rest his head in Roselle Park and he keep two muhfuckas wit' 'em, since that beef wit' them spaghetti heads. He done lost a lot of his closest people. These two Africans is like the last of his original team. They big, black, and trail that nigga like a shadow and they ready to die. So the only way we can get in on this cat is as satellite installers. She said she been buggin' the nigga for months to get one of them shits and now that this shit wit' her parents done went down, he feelin' guilty, buyin' the broad everything she want. Only problem," Ray paused for a moment before he dropped his bomb, "ain't no way we can get in strapped, so she gonna have two guns waitin' for us."

Craze and Dutch looked at each other like Ray was joking, and he could tell they didn't like what he had just said. Dutch had all kinds of thoughts running through his head. *This nigga must be tryin' something slick. I know he not trying to stick me.*

Ray took one look at Dutch and read his mind.

"Ahhh, naw, youngun, don't tell me you thinkin' like that. You thinkin' Sugar Ray done gave the rabbit the gun, huh? Come on, lil' nigga, even if I did, do you think Kazami would invite you to his house to dead you? Hell no, he'da been here waitin' on you when you got here, or better, he woulda gunned you down in the street like the rest of them muhfuckas."

Dutch looked at Ray. He was right. Craze looked around the apartment waiting for someone to jump out on him. That place could have easily been a death trap, and he could tell Dutch was thinking the same thing. When Ray saw they understood his point, he continued.

"Now, back to this installation shit. Man, this nigga been hit on twice, so he paranoid. Muhfuckin' Jehovah's Witness can't even get too close to this nigga with too many Bibles in they hand, so we lucky the bitch wanted satellite television."

"Yeah, you got a point, but going in this cat's house unarmed, dependin' on his chick to gun us?" Dutch just shook his head.

Ray leaned back in his chair, kicked his feet up, and said, "It's the only way. Shit, you think I want to go up in this crazy nigga's house without no gun? Hell no, but the broad wide open. She's gonna do what I tell her. You can take that to the bank wit' cha, youngun."

"What you think?" Dutch turned to Craze.

"I'm sayin', Ray right, ain't no way we gonna hit him this lovely nowhere else. Like you told me in Roberto's van that night, ain't no turning back now, 'cause we ain't got nowhere to go," Craze concluded.

"Set it up," he said to Ray.

A week later, they pulled up to the door of Kazami's house in an all-white stolen van. The house wasn't large, but it was definitely in good taste and extremely expensive. It sat back in a low-key section of Roselle Park, an area made up of mostly retired white folk. Craze drove with Dutch in the passenger seat and Ray in the back.

"There it is." Sugar Ray pointed.

Dutch didn't say a word, just glanced over at Craze, grabbed the toolbox, slid open the back door, and got out. He turned to Craze, who sat in the driver's seat with his nine-millimeter on his lap.

"You got ten minutes. After that, I'm comin' in." Then he held up his gun and looked at his watch.

Dutch smiled and winked at him, then turned and walked away.

"Let me handle the door, i-ight?" Ray demanded more than asked.

Dutch eyed Ray closely, then slowly nodded.

"Don't worry, youngun, I done talked us this far, right?"

Dutch didn't answer him. They climbed the stairs and Ray rang the doorbell. Dutch glanced around to survey the scenery. A black Lincoln sat in the driveway along with a silver convertible Jaguar. Up the block an elderly white man was watering his lawn. Dutch looked back at the van and saw no sign of Craze, who had reclined in the passenger seat out of sight.

After a few moments, the door opened and a large black man silently filled the door frame and stood there. Ray looked at the clipboard he had under his arm, then looked up at the huge black man.

"Umm, Mr. Carter?" asked Ray.

"Who you?" the big African replied.

"Look, evidently you ain't Mr. Carter, 'cause if you was, you'd know I'm from Universal Installations. Mr. Carter ordered a satellite," Ray said, feigning annoyance and nodding to the satellite box.

The African looked at Dutch, then at Ray, then at the satellite box.

"Open it," he ordered.

"Huh?"

"I said open it! Open the box!" he said, then made a move as if he were going to open it himself.

"Hold up, big man. I don't mean no harm, but until I know if you're Mr. Carter or not, that there don't belong to you, i-ight."

The large African man just eyed Ray, hard. "Wait here," he said, then slammed the door and relocked it. Dutch looked at Ray, who winked at him. A few short seconds later, the African returned with the most beautiful woman Dutch had ever seen.

Simone.

His heart skipped beats as his eyes traveled along every curve and contour of the ebony princess. He knew right away why Kazami had such a weakness for this beautiful creature, and he decided right there never to let a woman get as close to him as Simone was to Kazami.

She looked at Dutch and smiled knowingly at his open admiration for her, then turned to Ray. Recognition flashed in her eyes and her pupils dilated at the sight of Sugar Ray, her coconspirator.

"Now, I know you aren't Mr. Carter," Ray smoothly remarked.

"No, not quite. I'm his wife. I ordered the satellite."

"Now we're getting somewhere," Ray said.

Simone stood aside to let Sugar Ray and Dutch pass into the foyer. Ray picked up the satellite box, then he and Dutch crossed the threshold, past the point of no return. Dutch knew it was do or die.

They made it no farther than the foyer when the African repeated his earlier order.

"Now, open it."

Ray opened the box to reveal the satellite and its control unit. "Happy?"

"And the toolbox," the man said to Dutch.

"Man, what is with you?" Ray asked as the African just glanced at Ray as he checked out the toolbox.

After that, he reached for Ray to frisk him down, but Ray stepped back, "Hol' up, partna. I don't know what you into, but we ain't no toolbox," Ray said, looking at Simone questioningly.

"It's just formality. My husband is a very important man. So this is just routine for everyone."

Ray sighed loudly then turned his back to the man and raised his arms. After Ray, he frisked Dutch, then nodded to Simone.

"Come on, I'll show you where I want it at."

Ray could tell by her tone she wasn't talking about the satellite. He picked up the box, and he and Dutch followed Simone while the bodyguard followed them. They walked down a short hall then made a left into a large living room. On the couch was another bodyguard, shorter and bulkier than the first. Next to him, bent over, was the man they had come to see, sniffing lines of coke off a small mirror.

Kazami.

Dutch had never seen him this close before. He was silked from head to toe, with the diamond in his ear reflecting a spectrum of bluish light. His hands wore only two rings, but around his neck was the biggest piece Dutch had ever seen. Two intertwining full-body dragons with rubies for eyes and diamonds for fangs hung from a cablelike, nuggeted gold rope. His eyes were glued to the chain until Kazami raised his head. He wiped the powder from the tip of his nose and looked up, annoyed.

"Who the fuck is this?" he asked belligerently, in a Nigerian accent.

"They're here to put in the satellite, baby," Simone said, her voice dripping with honey. To Dutch, however, her words seemed dipped in poison.

"Yeah, well, hurry the hell up," Kazami grumbled, then turned his attention back to his mirror.

"Where do you want this, ma'am?" Ray asked after he cleared his throat.

"Right over here," she told them.

"You see I'm busy, damn. Put that shit in the bedroom or somethin'," Kazami said as he raised his head.

" 'Cause I don't want it in the bedroom. I want it in here. They ain't gonna be but a minute. Why you can't take that shit upstairs anyway? First you say I can get it, now you act li—"

"I-ight, i-ight, goddamn. Just hurry the fuck up," Kazami said, cutting her off, tired of her nagging, which was blowing his high. He got up and left the room with his bodyguard right behind him.

"I'm sorry about that. That's the TV right there I want it hooked to," she said, referring to the big-screen TV in the corner.

Ray opened the satellite box, took out the control unit, and carried it over to the TV. Dutch followed him carrying the toolbox. When they got to the TV, Ray looked behind it and saw a .45 automatic and a snub-nosed .38. He smiled up at Simone.

"Right here?"

"Yup, there," she said, smiling seductively at the guns lying on the floor.

"Partna, come take a look at this," said Sugar Ray, acting like he was working. "I ain't gonna show you how to hook this thing up no more. And grab that toolbox."

Dutch just looked at him, approaching with the toolbox in hand. Then he saw the guns and had to fight back the rush of adrenaline that hit him. Ray slid in farther behind the TV and began to unplug the wires from the VCR, arbitrarily. He put the .45 in the toolbox and took out a screwdriver, closing the box.

"Now, once you've hooked up the auxiliary cable to the transmitter . . ." Ray explained, using phrases at random, not knowing what the fuck he was talking about.

"You take this blue wire, which is the ground wire, and hook it to the C output." He acted like he was doing something and plugged a wire from the VCR into the control unit. "Now, you go outside and set the satellite up like I showed you on the last installation."

Dutch nodded, grabbed the toolbox, and lifted the satellite box.

"I'll walk you out," Simone offered.

The bodyguard watched Simone and Dutch walk out of the living room.

"You got it?" Simone asked as they turned the corner.

Dutch pulled the .45 out of the toolbox and checked the clip.

"Yeah." He smiled.

"He's upstairs," she whispered, looking over her shoulder furtively.

"Go unlock the front door and leave it open," he said. She nodded, and he watched her hurry to the door, almost regretting the fate her treachery had bought her.

Part of the game, he thought to himself as he saw Craze tiptoe in the door, gun in hand. Dutch pointed upstairs, then jerked his head for Craze to follow. They tiptoed down the hall, back to the living room door. Dutch peeped around the corner into the living room to see where the bodyguard was. Ray had him squatting next to him by the TV talking about satellite installation, even though Ray himself didn't know what he was doing.

Dutch and Craze hurried by, then slowly headed up the stairs. Nearing the top, they heard voices. They traveled down a long hallway, peering in each open door they passed. They heard the sound of a toilet flushing, and Dutch nodded to Craze to go ahead of him.

Dutch looked into the next room and saw Kazami standing with his back to him bending over a baby's playpen. Dutch looked down the hall at Craze up against the wall. He pointed to himself then turned the corner into the baby's room.

"Kazami," Dutch articulated slowly, savoring each syllable.

Kazami spun around quickly at the unfamiliar voice. His eyes widened at the sight of Dutch and the .45 barrel pointed at him.

"Don't scream, don't yell, don't even fuckin' breathe, or I'll send your son where his grandfather went," Dutch stated firmly.

"Wh-what do you want?" Kazami stammered.

"You, but if you cooperate, I'll settle for the money." Dutch gave Kazami his trademark smile.

"Who sent you?"

Dutch was impressed with how quickly Kazami regained

his composure. But he knew Kazami was a thoroughbred too, and Dutch imagined himself reacting the same way if he were in the same predicament.

"That's not important, but steppin' away from the crib is," Dutch ordered.

Kazami backed away, watching as Dutch picked up his small child. Dutch never took his eyes or the gun off Kazami. When the child was safely in his arms, Dutch arrogantly lowered the gun to the baby's side while cradling the child in comfort.

"Please, please, man, please don't hurt my son," Kazami begged. But because of his cold heart, Dutch didn't see a caring father . . . only a weak man.

"Of course not. I mean, why should I when his father is so cooperative?" Dutch responded as he kissed the child.

Just then, Dutch heard a muffled thump. Craze appeared at the door with the bodyguard down on all fours and a gun to his head.

"I got his dog on a leash," Craze whispered as he saw Dutch. "Who's the baby?" Craze asked, knowing his best friend too well.

"Let's go downstairs. You and your dog first," Dutch told Kazami. The bodyguard stood up slowly, and he and Kazami descended the stairs with Craze and Dutch, still holding the baby, behind them. Simone saw them as they entered the living room, and Kazami could see by the look in her eyes that she was the one who had brought all this about.

In a rage, he forgot about the danger he was in and rushed Simone, smacking her to the floor. "Fuckin' bitch! You did this! You!"

The bodyguard with Ray turned around in surprise. But

before he could react, Craze stepped forward and fired twice into his chest, dropping him as Kazami, Simone, and the entire room fell silent.

"Hold up, Craze. Let's everybody be cool, i-ight," Dutch said, looking at Kazami as he snuggled his son.

Simone slowly stood up, catching her balance, holding her bruised and swollen face, while Kazami glared at her with death in his eyes.

"Everybody get down on the floor!" Dutch suddenly announced, waving his gun around as they all kneeled down. The bodyguard Craze had shot moaned out his last breath. Ray pulled out the other .38 and stood up with Craze and Dutch.

"Now we gonna keep this real simple. Niggas here for the money, all of it. If you try and hold back as much as a fuckin' wooden nickel, I'll turn this baby into Swiss cheese," Dutch said, emphasizing his point by putting the gun to the child's head.

"What are you talkin' about? What the hell are you doing?" Simone questioned, jumping up to aid her baby, who was in danger. "Ray, stop him, tell him to give me my baby!" Simone cried.

"Don't worry, sugar, ain't nothin' changed. Let's just go get the money and get this here over wit'. Dutch . . . he ain't gonna hurt your son," Ray assured her. But he glanced at Dutch nervously, because he knew what the man was capable of.

"Listen to him, baby girl. Go 'head and get that," Dutch said to Simone as he turned to Craze, "Go wit' 'em."

Craze looked at the faces of Kazami and the other bodyguard, seeing the motors in their minds spinning at breakneck speed, waiting for an opportunity to turn the tables.

"You straight in here with them two?" Craze asked.

Dutch looked at Craze, then at the bodyguard. The guard returned Dutch's nonchalant gaze with a hard stare. Dutch stepped closer and shot the guard in the head, point-blank range. The baby began to cry at the sound of gunfire filling the air. The bodyguard slumped to the carpet.

"Yeah, I'll be i-ight," Dutch said, turning to Craze, then back to the baby. "Shhh, hush now, it's okay. Uncle Dutch got you," he said as he bounced the baby gently and watched Simone, Ray, and Craze leave the room.

"You got a fly lil' cat here, Duke. What's his name?"

"Please, man, just take the money. Just take it and go," Kazami pleaded, trying to sound as authoritative as his precarious situation would allow him. Dutch ignored him and again started talking to the baby, who had calmed down in Dutch's embrace.

"Look at you, you a big boy? You a big boy like your daddy, ain't you? You know who your daddy is? Kazami, the African who was untouchable. Yo' daddy is a big man, even the mob couldn't catch him," Dutch told the baby as he turned the child around to see his father. "Now look at 'im."

The little baby boy reached out his arms to Kazami and blurted happily, "Daddy!"

Dutch laughed as he saw the pain and agony in Kazami's eyes and wondered how such a weak man could be feared for so long. Kazami had commitments that made him weak and Dutch had none, which made him stronger.

"What do you think I should do? 'Cause you know you gonna die, right? Of course you do. But I tell you what I'm gonna do for you, like one last favor. I'ma let you kill yo' ho.

You like that? I know you know she got you set up. I seen the way you flipped on her, and since I respect the game, I'ma let you handle you," Dutch said as Kazami eyed him curiously. "So when my man comes back, I'm gonna hand you a gun, deal?"

Kazami didn't know what to think.

"Yo-you . . . you gonna give me a gun?"

"Why not? You kill her, then I kill you. Of course I could do it. I'll blast the bitch then blast the kid, then blast you, but you don't want that, do you, Zami? It's truly a once-in-a-lifetime offer," Dutch said, smiling at him.

Kazami dropped his head in defeat and slowly shook it, no.

"Okay then, so we got a deal or what?"

"Yeah . . . yeah, we got a deal."

"I-ight now, I'ma hold you to your word and if I think you tryin' some funny shit, I'll make it so you'll have to bury this kid in a cup," Dutch threatened, meaning every word.

The tears began to creep down Kazami's cheeks. He knew the man in front of him was colder, hungrier, and sharper than he was. He knew this young wolf wouldn't hesitate to do what he said. Kazami knew it was over. He knew this man would take his life, and his only revenge would be knowing that Simone would pay with her life, for her deception.

Simone and Sugar Ray entered the room with Craze, who was carrying a bulging garbage bag. Kazami's eyes blazed with rage when he saw Simone, and she returned his stare with a defiant smirk etched on her face.

"Check this, Craze. While y'all was gone, me and Zami over here made a deal. Didn't we, Zami? Nothin' major, just a lil' surprise for Simone here. So check this, Ray. How 'bout you give Zami yo' joint," said Dutch.

"Give him what? Nigga, is you crazy? Give him . . . Craze, what the fuck is wrong wit' this nigga?" Sugar Ray exclaimed.

"Ray, Ray, calm down, man. Didn't you say you couldn't trust the bitch? If this ho set you up, wouldn't you want some get back, too? Least we can do is give the nigga that much. Respect the game, baby," Dutch told him.

Simone's head started turning from side to side as she listened to Dutch, her eyes widening with fear at his every word. Trembling, she turned to Ray. "Ray, baby, what is he talkin' 'bout? You can trust me, I swear you can!" Simone was terrified.

She tried to hug Ray. Ray just looked down at her hanging on his neck, then at Kazami, then finally at Dutch. It was at that moment that he started to fear Dutch himself. Dutch was a madman and Ray wanted no part of him anymore.

He handed the gun to Kazami. Simone watched as the piece of metal exchanged palms. As Kazami took the gun, Simone tried to run out of the room. Craze stopped her, grabbed her by the hair, and threw her back in front of Kazami.

"No, Ojee, please! Let me explain, please, I love you!"

The audacity of her plea, the madness of the moment, and the hurt of betrayal filled Kazami beyond capacity. He raised the gun, pulled the trigger, and hit Simone in the chest. The baby screamed at the sound and sight of his dying mother, but Kazami fired again into her head. She lay lifeless in a pool of her own blood, nerves still twitching.

"Now before you give the gun back, I want you to meet

my man, Sugar Ray. See, Sugar Ray, he the type of man no woman can resist, they love this nigga. Don't they, Sugar Ray?"

It was at that moment Sugar Ray knew he had made the worst mistake of his life. He had never thought Dutch would kill him, but faced with the reality, he saw it all too clearly. He was the link between the hits, and he cursed himself for not seeing it before.

"Dutch! Come on, man! What you doin'? Craze," he said turning to Craze with a plea for mercy in his eyes. He knew Craze was the only one who could stop Dutch, but Craze shrugged his shoulders as if there was nothing he could do for him. Ray turned back to Dutch while Craze kept his gun on Kazami.

"Don't do this, Dutch, man, please. Is it the money? It's all there—take it man, it's yours. Just don't do me like this."

"Come on, Ray. You remember fifty-fifty? Partnas? I can't take your dough. Man, you earned that. Tell Kazami how you sang his girl to sleep and set all this up. Even got on Kazami's ring. Go 'head, show him," spoke Dutch calmly as he instigated. Ray stared at him coldly.

"Show him," repeated Dutch as Kazami looked at Ray's hand and saw his ring. "Yeah, Zami, it's yours. The bitch who shared yo' bed, who bore your son, was behind your back, suckin' Ray's dick, takin' it, lovin' it, and comin' home drippin' his nut. Goddamn, nigga, you got the gun—fuck you gonna do?" Dutch urged as Kazami raised the gun. Ray turned to Dutch and smoothly drawled his last words.

"I'll see you in hell, nigga."

The blast caught him high in the chest and he crumpled to the carpet. Before Dutch could move, Kazami turned the gun on himself. All in one motion, he raised the gun to his head and pulled the trigger. He fell beside Simone; his bloody head rested on her thigh.

"Damn!" Dutch said as he looked down on Kazami's lifeless body. "Fuck he do that for?"

"What you expect, the nigga to wait on you? Shouldn't have gave the nigga no gun no way."

"Now how we suppose to find the real paper he got stashed?"

"Serve yo' dumb ass right," Craze said as he held up the bag. "Ain't nothing but a couple hundred thousand in here."

Dutch cocked his head to one side, aggravated. His glance fell on two large swords above the fireplace, crossed in the shape of an X. He smiled, then handed the baby to Craze. Craze watched as he pulled the swords down and examined the blades.

"What you gonna do with that?"

Craze found out soon enough. Dutch rolled Simone's body away and took aim at Kazami's neck. After the second hack, Craze was forced to look away. It took several blows for Dutch to hack through the muscle and bone of Kazami's neck until his head finally detached. Dutch picked the head up and placed it in a bag with the money. He then turned back to Kazami's body and pulled the bloody dragon rope from Kazami's neck stump and slung it around his own neck.

"Now, we set this shit on fire," he told Craze.

"What about him?" Craze asked in a concerned tone, referring to the baby.

But Dutch didn't answer.

"Come on, son, it's a baby," Craze said as Dutch just looked at the baby, sighing

"All right, all right, just help me set this muhfucker on fire so we can get out of here."

They pulled out ten minutes later in the van, leaving the house ablaze. Flames leaped into the twilight sky. They left the baby on a neighbor's porch screaming for his parents as his home burned.

Craze watched the moon from the New Jersey parkway on their way back to Newark. It was the first time the moon seemed to follow him, as if it, too, had witnessed the night's atrocities. He glanced down at the garbage bag between his feet. It was more money than he had ever seen in his life, but it seemed he had sold his soul to get it.

He looked over at Dutch, who was driving quietly, focused only on the road. Craze wondered what was going through his mind. He loved Dutch like a brother and he wondered about him, but only sometimes.

Craze reached to turn on the radio. A cassette was playing Kool G Rap's "Road to the Riches." Craze turned the volume up as he and Dutch nodded to what would be their theme song.

Twenty minutes later, Dutch pulled up to Roberto's Pizzeria. Dutch went inside while Craze stayed in the car. A half hour passed before Dutch and Roberto walked out and got into Roberto's dark blue Riviera. Craze followed them as he glanced at the bag on the passenger-side floor. They drove into the Italian section of Newark and headed toward Fat Tony's restaurant, Sophia's. It was a large restaurant, complete with its own parking lot and outdoor patio area.

He followed Roberto around back to the service entrance and stopped. Dutch got out and came over to the passenger side of the car.

"Come on, leave your gun," he said as he grabbed the bag off the floor. Craze tossed his gun under the seat, then closed his car door. He followed Dutch and Roberto in through the service entrance.

Inside, the kitchen was busy with the rapid movements of waiters and chefs and the zesty aroma of Italian food. Roberto spoke in Italian to an elderly woman and stole a piece of sausage she was cutting. She hit his hand with the flat part of the knife and cursed him in Italian.

Roberto led them up a flight of stairs that led to a long, darkened hallway and ended at a set of double doors. He knocked and in moments the door was opened by a middle-aged Sicilian man with a long scar down the left side of his face.

Roberto spoke to him in Italian and the man let them in. They followed the man into a plush mahogany and leather interior office where two more Italians sat on the couch. Fat Tony sat behind his desk, puffing a cigar.

Dutch looked at the two guys on the couch, who sneered at him with hard and steady eyes. One of the men, whom he didn't know at the time, was a man he'd come to know well . . .

Frank Sorbonno.

Dutch and Craze kept a respectful distance from Tony's desk while Roberto went up to Tony and shook his hand.

"Dutch, is that you, kid?" asked Tony.

"Yeah, Mr. Cerone, it's me, and this is my man, Chris," Dutch answered.

"Well, come the fuck over here, let me look at cha. It's been a long time, huh?" Tony jovially remarked.

Dutch walked up to Tony, carrying the garbage bag, and shook his hand.

"You lookin' good, I see. Prison brought the man outta ya, huh? That's good, 'cause sometimes it'll bring out the bitch, if there's any there. But you, look at the shoulders, huh?" joked Tony, his heavy chuckle shaking his gut. "How you been?"

"Can't complain," responded Dutch.

Tony nodded as he surveyed Dutch, then glanced down at the bag he was holding. "What's that?"

Dutch looked at Tony silently until Tony got the message.

"Frank, this here's Dutch, an old friend of mine. Gimme a sec, will ya?" asked Fat Tony of his two guests on the couch.

Frank reluctantly nodded and slowly got up. He and the other man walked by Craze, eyeing him condescendingly, then exited. The doorman looked at Tony, who nodded in his direction, and he too walked out of the room, closing the door behind him.

"So what's up wit' the stone face, kid? Where's that smile my grandma would die for?"

"You had a problem and I solved it, now I got a problem," Dutch explained.

Tony sat back and puffed his cigar before tapping his ashes. "I'm an old man, Dutch, and I don't do so good wit' riddles, so ahhh, what's the problem?"

Dutch looked back at Craze, then at Tony. He set the garbage bag on the edge of the desk and began to peel down the bag until Kazami's decapitated head came into full view. The sight of Kazami's head made Tony jump out of his seat and drop his cigar.

"Jesus! Are you fuckin' crazy? You bring a fuckin' head in my fuckin' restaurant? Roberto, what the fuck is wrong with this kid?" asked Tony as he sat back down and picked up his cigar. "Put that shit away," he added as he relit the cigar. "I take it this is part of your problem, huh?"

Dutch nodded, as he covered the head back up, but left the bag on the table.

"So who is it anyway?"

"Kazami."

Tony's jaw dropped as one word came out. "Who?"

"Your problem—I said I solved it," Dutch responded.

Tony thought how Frank had tried to kill the Nigerian twice, missing both times, and Tony wondered to himself how the hell the young kid in front of him had managed to pull it off.

"So, ahh, I'm sure you didn't just find it rollin' down the street?" Tony signified, trying to lure Dutch into a play by play.

"Naw, let's just say it fell in my lap." Dutch smiled.

"Fell in his lap," Tony repeated, laughing hard. "You hear this fuckin' guy, Roberto? Where'd you get this kid, Roberto?"

"Sweeping floors," Roberto said as he shrugged his shoulders.

Craze finally relaxed at the sound of the men's laughter. He had never been in the company of Fat Tony or men of his ilk, so he didn't know what to expect. But he knew laughter was a good sign, although he still didn't fully understand what Dutch was here for.

"So, Dutch, you bring me a fuckin' head in a bag, set it on my desk, and tell me you got a problem. Now, I suppose this is the part where you ask me to solve it?" Tony concluded.

Dutch didn't answer. He again dug in the bag and began to take out stack after stack of money and began placing it in neat rows in front of Tony's greedy eyes. He continued to produce stacks until he felt Tony's greed was appeased for what he was about to present.

"That's a helluva bag, kid. What else you got in there?" Tony joked.

"Mr. Cerone, I know this ain't much to a man like you, but it's all I got right now. It's at least a hundred grand there. Consider it a gift from me and Kazami."

Tony looked at Dutch and then at the money. He picked up a stack and examined the blood traces that gilded the edges and corners. *Now this is real blood money,* he thought to himself.

"Mr. Cerone, I saw an opportunity and I took it, just like I did three years ago. I told you I did it then 'cause I consider Roberto a friend and I know he wouldn't have brought me here if he didn't consider me one. So what I ask from you is simple . . . your friendship," Dutch finished and looked Tony in his eyes.

Tony nodded with understanding, knowing his friendship meant protection. He looked up at Roberto and then down at the stacks of money Dutch had laid before him. He rose from his chair and walked over to a large glass window overlooking the streets. He measured the gravity of Dutch's request. Dutch had taken the streets and was asking for his support in keeping them.

He thought of the ambitious and conniving Frank Sorbonno. They were Frank's hits, because Frank wanted in on the drug trade in Newark. Tony had never had an interest in drugs or drug money. He considered it too messy. But to back this little black kid over Frank would show Frank what he really thought of him. He didn't like Frank. In fact, he despised him because he knew Frank wanted to be where he was. But Tony was made and Frank wasn't, so there was little chance of that. He decided to use this situation to further distance himself from Frank, show him who was boss, and rake in the money all with one nod.

"So, you wanna be the boss, huh? It takes more than balls to be the boss. You think 'cause you kill the head, the body will die? Not in this game it don't. Everybody wants to be chief and there's not enough Indians. You see that head in the bag over there? You think it can't happen to you?" asked Tony.

"Anybody can get it, but I promise you, I'ma live till I die."

"Well, then you got a friend as long as you live," said Tony as he extended his hand. Dutch gripped it firmly. There were no more words exchanged between men that night, nothing else needed to be said.

Craze thought back to that night when the streets became theirs. They had done the impossible and come out on top. From that day on, they reigned untouchable . . .

But look at us now. Zoom's dead, Roc and Angel are in prison, and Qwan was on the stand, turning state. He shook his head in disbelief.

"Times done really changed," he said to himself and got back into his Porsche.

CHAPTER NINE

♦

ANGEL'S SONG

Finished with her day's work in the prison kitchen, Angel walked to her cell and sat down on her bunk. She kicked off her boots and reached for the pack of Newports on her little desk. She put one in her mouth and struck a match just as her cellmate came running into the cell with a copy of the *Daily News*.

"You seen this?" her celly asked and handed her the paper.

Angel hadn't seen the *Daily News* in a few months. Danbury, Connecticut, was a long way from Newark, New Jersey. However, several inmates, her roommate included, had subscriptions to hometown newspapers to keep up with their temple of familiarities while they did time. Angel had no temple to contemplate, so the *Daily News* was the furthest thing from her mind. But seeing Dutch on the cover walking out of the courtroom piqued her interest.

The headline read: "Gangster Chronicles Continue." She gazed at Dutch's black-and-white photo, the drabness of the colorless flick taking nothing away from the smile he wore. Confident . . . arrogant . . . Dutch.

Her celly stood in the doorway waiting for Angel to hand

her back the paper, but when she saw how she was just staring at the picture, she merely sighed.

"Just give it back when you're through," said the girl, then she walked out.

Angel hadn't heard a word she said. She was too preoccupied with the newspaper, looking at Dutch from every angle, even looking at all the people around him. She memorized the photo, then laid the paper aside, got up, and looked out her small cell window.

The rain fell in torrents, making everything outside a gray blur. She sat back on the bed and lit another match. After she lit her cigarette, she lay back on her bunk and placed a hand behind her head. In the distance, thunder boomed as she stared at the cold white of the cell's ceiling. *Life in prison, how I'm suppose to do life?* she thought to herself, then took a long drag on the cigarette. She hadn't been down a year and couldn't fathom the rest of her life and what the years behind bars would bring.

She had one of the best criminal lawyers filing her appeal, but it would be a long, hard fight. She thought back to the interrogation tactics they used on her.

"You know you're going to jail?"

"Prison."

"A pretty girl like you, mmm, damn shame, too."

"So, tell us what we want to know."

It took some time before they realized that she wasn't a weak link, but the actual cement to Dutch's solid brick structure. When the sweet, caring approach didn't work they began to figure out that Angel was only her name and not her nature. That's when they applied force.

"You're gonna fry for this, you hear me?"

"You think that son of a bitch would be doin' this for you?"

"You can't be that stupid."

The interrogation lasted for days and nights, but Angel never cracked. She kept a sarcastic charm and feigned ignorance in response to all their questions, and when all else failed, her final response was, "Man, you can suck my dick!"

When the feds realized she wouldn't cooperate, their final words were, "So, you wanna wear it, huh? Well, we're gonna make sure it fits . . . tight!"

The trial should've been held in a kangaroo court, because with one crooked leap and a single unjust bound, Angel stood before a judge and heard the words "life without parole" cast down upon her young head.

She was twenty-six.

When she was sentenced, she didn't become belligerent or befuddled. She simply mouthed a silent "fuck you" to the judge, who nodded and smirked devilishly back at her before banging his gavel and ending the trial.

She crushed the Newport butt in the ashtray that rested on her stomach. She thought about the night she was arrested along with Roc. The same night they got knocked, Zoom got killed.

It was around the same time that Roc's wife, Ayesha, was in the hospital in labor with their third child. Of the whole crew, Roc was the only one who had a wife, or even a steady girl, for that matter. After seeing what happened to Kazami, nobody was really into broads and babies, except for Roc.

But then, Ayesha had been with Roc since before Dutch even knew him.

Zoom and Angel had taken Roc out to celebrate the birth of his new baby. They had stopped by one of Dutch's after-hours lounges he had tucked away on the low and left with a case of Henny. They were riding in Zoom's S600 when Roc's phone rang. Angel and Zoom could tell by Roc's conversation that he was obviously not where he was supposed to be. He had told Ayesha before that there was no way he was doing that baby thing ever again after seeing the way the first one came out of her vagina.

"Ain't no way I'll be there for the next one."

"Ain't gon' be no next one, nigga," she playfully responded.

But Ayesha was wrong. However, Roc wasn't, because he was riding and wasn't going to that hospital and he didn't care which one of Ayesha's family members rang his phone.

"Zoom, what you 'posed to say 'bout a murder-type nigga who can dead twelve niggas before dinner, but scared of a pussy!" Angel laughed. "I told y'all the nigga was bitch!"

Zoom and Angel laughed while Roc emptied his second bottle of Hennessy to the head.

"Y'all can call me what the fuck y'all want, that shit opened up like a wide-ass door," Roc remarked, dead-ass serious.

They arrived at the hospital completely drunk, laughing and joking as they entered the emergency doors. They made their way to the paternity ward after Angel had cursed out two nurses and cracked on a third. When they got to the room, Ayesha was sitting up in her bed, her sister, Jamillah, next to her eating an apple.

"Where you been?" she asked angrily.

Roc stumbled over to her and tried to kiss her on the lips.

"And you drunk? You must be crazy, nigga! I'm in here cryin' my eyes out tryin' to get your baby out me and you runnin' 'round galavantin' with your friends?" Ayesha pushed him off her and looked at him with wide eyes, shaking her head in disgust.

"Naw, boo, check it," Roc slurred, then tried to touch her face as she smacked his hand away.

"Naw, boo, shit! My whole family was here, but not you! What the fuck is that shit? You don't even care. No tellin' where the fuck you been," she said, looking like she was ready to either burst into tears or fight.

Roc stood up straight as he could, wobbling a little, but sobering up quick. He turned to Zoom and Angel.

"Ay, yo, y'all wait outside, i-ight."

They complied and began to exit as Roc saw Jamillah still sitting in her chair, munching on her apple.

"You is y'all, too," he said giving her the boogly boogly eyes.

"This is my sister's room. You don't be tellin' me to get out!" Jamillah spat, her head rolling like it was about to come off.

Ayesha looked at Jamillah and Jamillah got the message. She got up, rolled her eyes at Roc, and went out the door.

All three of them stood there and listened to Ayesha curse out Roc. Roc attempted to reply. He was a deadly brother, but he respected women, especially his wife. Angel had heard them argue like that for years. So this was nothing new. Ten minutes later, Roc came out of the hospital room sober, as if the visit with Ayesha was a big, strong, black cup of coffee.

"Y'all ready?" he snapped.

"Nigga, don't come out here and be gangster after coppin' pleas in there," Zoom said, standing up as everybody laughed at Roc.

"I know. I don't know who this nigga think he be talkin' to, right, Zoom?" said Angel, smacking high fives with Zoom.

Outside the hospital, walking to the car, a breeze caught Angel and a sensation made her grip the butt of the pistol she carried at her waist.

"What's wrong with you?" Roc asked.

Shaking her head, Angel just looked around the crowded parking lot, "Nothin'."

They walked across the lot to the S600, and as Zoom pressed his ignition key to unlock the doors, an unmarked federal car skidded up as two other cars threw on lights and lit up the parking lot. It seemed as if federal agents were everywhere.

"Freeze! Get down on the ground! Now!"

The feds had waited too long to make their move. Angel, followed by Roc and Zoom, pulled out their weapons and began to open fire as they ran between parked cars toward the S600.

Bullets ricocheted, barely missing her as she dove into the backseat of Zoom's car. She turned around as she saw an agent firing his weapon at Roc. The agent's gun was aimed straight for Roc's back, and Angel could see the bullet in slow motion hit its target. Roc's eyes opened wide, and he bellowed in agony as he looked at her, collapsing face-first on the ground.

Zoom slammed the driver's door as he saw Roc go down. He screeched away from his parking spot, hopped the curb, and drove down the sidewalk until he got to an opening where no car was parked and skidded into the street.

Accompanied by Newark narcs, the remaining federal agents followed in hot pursuit although they would have been no match for Zoom's inner-city driving skills . . . had he been sober.

Angel learned the wisdom of Dutch's ways that night: He had always stressed no drugs and no drinking. But it was too late to take heed. Zoom tried to lock the Benz up and split two oncoming cars but he misjudged and was sideswiped by the second car. The S600 careened into a parked car and crashed head-on into a fire hydrant.

Angel, who was in the backseat, was instantly knocked unconscious. Suspended between consciousness and unconsciousness, she could vaguely hear the shouts of muffled voices and far-off gunshots. She later found out that Zoom had emerged from the car, firing against the law as he tried to escape. He shot and killed two agents before being shot in the back of the head and in his spine, dead before he hit the pavement.

Roc lay facedown on the concrete in the parking lot, bleeding from the gunshot wound. The federal agents handcuffed him behind his back and left him lying on the ground for over an hour before calling an ambulance. He passed out several times from pain and loss of blood, but to the feds' dismay, he didn't die.

Angel lay on her mat thinking how fate would deem her fortunate, or unfortunate, depending on how you looked at it. Had she not been unconscious that night, surely she would have battled to her death, just like Zoom. She would've seen to it. No way would she have chosen prison over death. Fuck an appeal. But the decision was not hers; it was made for her. She wondered why God had opted to spare her that night. Was it another chance or just torture for the life she had led, the lives she had taken . . . the lives she had ruined.

She looked back at the newspaper's picture again. She had only been worried about Dutch twice in her life—the night they killed Kazami and now.

"I don't care what you say, I'm going."

"Come on, ma. You know the plan. You, Roc, and Qwan will hit the safehouse in Newark, while Zoom and the Zoo Crew hit the one in Elizabeth at the same time, no matter what, you hear me?"

"What if something happens to you? Then what?"

"Then y'all some rich niggas," said Dutch, as if he was predicting the future.

The safehouses were easy targets, because none of Kazami's people expected or were ready to be hit. They were running their operation based on reputation, since everyone feared Kazami and his wild African organization. Everyone, that is, except Dutch.

That night they came back with over twenty kilos of heroin . . . and became millionaires in less than a few hours. Angel sat and waited for Dutch and Craze to return. Nervously, she paced and thought the worst until they walked through the door, Dutch wearing the massive medallion that had once belonged to Kazami, not to mention his bag, which she later learned the contents of.

The celebration that ensued lasted for three days and four nights before it was time to move into the final phase of consolidating Kazami's organization. That phase became known as the Month of Murder. Within twenty-seven days, sixty-three people were killed. The majority of those individuals were remnants of Kazami's Nigerian force, and the rest were other hungry young teams of wolves that Dutch knew would try to come out in the melee to take part in the free fall of the streets. So before they even thought about it, Dutch shut them down.

It was like a military coup in some third world country, except that the country was the streets and Dutch was the army. Dutch had niggas gunned down wherever they stood, and then had his clean-up teams of youngsters invade wakes, funerals, and hospitals to finish off whoever was left.

The heroin was distributed by Dutch, to outfitted operations with enough guns for guerilla warfare and enough jewels to draw the envy of ancient Mayan kings.

Despite Fat Tony's connections in the police and political arena, the cops were heated and haters. Too much paper for one black man to be getting, so there was heat. But Dutch had that covered, too. He opened up after-hours spots from Linden to Jersey City.

He would convert abandoned three-family homes in quiet neighborhoods into hot gambling and liquor dens. He sectioned off the floors. The basement was for card games or dice games. The first floor was the bar and kitchen. The second floor was reserved room by room for VIPs of the club who were entertained by dancers Dutch employed, who wore half of nothing.

The attic was the lookout, where vigil was kept for raids and stickups. It was like being the Maytag man in the commercials. With Fat Tony's protection from law enforcement and the fear Dutch had instilled in the grain of the streets, raids and hits were highly unlikely.

And as Dutch planned, the spots were his way to keep his ear to the streets. Everybody who was anybody came through. Rappers, sports figures, and the nation's biggest hustlers all came like it was Vegas, and the smallest scramblers frequented the spots too, trying to catch the crumbs of the fortunate and bask in the light of the players.

Angel's job was easy. She never had to touch heroin again. Her job was to play and trick on the customers. She would gather information off the streets through the pillow in the freaks. Angel was a bad bitch. She had broads working for her, running for her, fucking niggas for her, sticking niggas up for her—the whole nine. She called her clique Angel's Charlies. And Diamond was her angel, her first lover at the age of fifteen. Diamond was older and more mature about her desire for pussy, calling it just that.

"I can't help thinking about sucking your pussy, Angel. Can I?" she asked as she bent down and kissed Angel's lips.

Angel didn't need to answer. The moment that she had been waiting for had finally come. While she was too shy to approach the subject, Diamond did what Angel was afraid to do: make a move. And Angel never looked back.

All the girls whom Angel met and fucked through Diamond were young, beautiful, and deadly, moving with drugs, pussy, and paper, moving in silence. All down with getting money and playing positions. There was no way to know who were Charlies and who weren't, and Dutch loved them all, sometimes all together.

Angel stood up and stretched her arms over her head, then checked her watch. It was almost chow time.

She leaned over the table to grab another cigarette and looked at the picture of her and Dutch. It was the only photo she had in her cell of just the two of them. It was her twenty-first birthday, a night she'd never forget.

Dutch had rented a club in Manhattan called Kilimanjaro's for a private birthday party. Private in the sense of exclusive, because it was far from intimate. Ghetto superstars from Brooklyn's notorious Kendu to Miguel Navarro and Peter Shue were in the house, along with Mike Tyson and rappers Heavy D, Craig Mack, and some kid from the Same Gang who got hold of the mic and wouldn't let that shit go.

Faith sang like a hummingbird, a beautiful happy birthday melody, for Dutch, 'cause she didn't know Angel, and an unknown group from Staten Island that we'd later know as the Wu Tang, was in the motherfucker tearing everything up. It was a party of all parties. Even the mayor sent twenty-one long-stemmed white roses, representing her age.

Dutch, Craze, two Charlies, and Angel were seated in a large corner booth while player after player and gangstress after gangstress lined up with good wishes and cards filled with currency or gifts in wrapped boxes. For the first time in her life she felt special, really special. She looked around the crowded room.

Craze was onstage performing, drunk, holding a bottle of Dom in his hand and some girl's ass in the other. Zoom and his Zoo Crew were out on the floor trying to get shorties to strip for hundred-dollar bills. Roc had come through with Ayesha. Dutch loved to see them together. It was a wonderful night. Dutch sat next to Angel, playing with her silliness, enjoying her drunkenness, and watching her every move. She even got him to drink.

"Come on, Dutch, do it for me, please," she whimpered like a sick puppy.

"I'm only doing this for you," he said, looking at her mouth open as he turned the bottle up and wondered if Angel could kiss or suck a dick.

"I wanna take a picture, come on."

"A picture?" he repeated, looking at her bending down on his kneecaps getting all in his face with her chest all in his view.

"Yeah, I'm only twenty-one once. I've known you my whole life, now, let's go," she said, pulling him up and out of the booth and toward the front of the club.

She and Dutch stood in front of a backdrop that read, in graffiti, "Happy Birthday Angel," as the photographer prepared to take the picture.

"You know, Dutch, you the only nigga I want to fuck me," she said as she quickly turned around and cheesed a big grin at the cameraman. The thought went through Dutch, hard.

She placed the picture back on the table, savoring the memory. It was her night to be a princess. What she had told him was true, too. Angel hated, or better yet, despised men. She didn't trust them, and while Dutch didn't trust women, they trusted each other, completely.

There was no second-guessing the lengths they would travel for each other. Angel was proving that by standing in the nine-by-seven cell she called home. She knew that there was no other woman who loved Dutch unconditionally like she did, no other woman, except for Nina.

CHAPTER TEN

◆

NINA'S ONLY NO

In the seven years since his release from prison, Dutch had accomplished more than most people do in a lifetime. He was only twenty-five at the pinnacle of his reign, diversifying from drugs into entertainment, restaurants, and fashion. Even his team at Rucker's Park seemed unbeatable.

Dutch couldn't lose, he wouldn't lose. He would always win. He was in charge of the streets and of everything that flowed through them and around them. He had everything, except a wife.

When it came to women, Dutch was much too choosy. He liked the complete package, complete. And although he had traveled all over the world, he still hadn't found her.

From Venice to Aspen, from Harrod's in London to the French Riviera, Dutch had his pick of the most exquisite women. For his enjoyment, he would take one with him to Nassau and dine at the Fish Fry or Negril, just to watch the sunset. Or he would fly another on a private jet to the French Riviera for a few days, then abandon her when he returned home.

Dutch always played fair with his women by letting them

know not to expect more than what he offered at that moment. He never lied about his intentions and never made false promises. He was a gentleman to those he chose to share his time and his bed with.

Dutch selected these women very carefully. They were strong women who could mentally challenge him, though none were on his level. He didn't want drama or fatal attractions, and damn . . . she's missing. So, he avoided jilted lovers and demanding femmes fatales. If a woman played by Dutch's rules, he would do anything for her. But if she didn't, he would end the game.

Dutch was six-three, muscular, with a handsome face and puppy dog eyes. He was proud of his unblemished, jet-black complexion and completely aware of his effect on the ladies. He could melt hearts with a glance and turn women to puddles of wetness without saying a word. Dutch's power of attraction never failed.

But she was different . . .

He had one rule: Never get involved in any way whatsoever with someone inside his sphere of influence or within the realm of his businesses.

But she was different . . .

He made his rounds to his after-hours spots, and had seen plenty of women who he wouldn't dare bother . . . dime joints, at that.

But she was different . . .

Plenty of women from all over the world, beautiful women like a breeze blew them from New Orleans, creole style. And, yes, his rule had been strained, but never broken. And, yes, his willpower had been tested by physical attraction and lust, but only in his mind.

But she was different . . .

His heart was lonely for love, even though he wasn't, and it had been like that all his adult life. He said he'd never let anyone in. He said he'd never let anyone get too close.

But she was different.

She was at one of the card tables gambling on spades. Her skin was the color of Camay, if Camay had been born brown. She radiated, and her skin glowed. She was surrounded by the Tri-States' best-looking women, yet she didn't have to compete with anyone. She merely succeeded where others failed without even trying.

Dutch inched closer to the table to get a chance to hear her speak.

"Y'all went what?" she said as she looked in her hand and recounted.

"I got one and a pimp, Nina," said her partner, staring at some Puerto Rican cutie, drenched in ice, over at the bar.

"Hello? Tamika! Girl, is you playin' or what? Shit, I got money on this and you over there ho'n?"

"Hold up, that nigga's about to leave. I'll be right back," Tamika said, running off toward the door.

"Look at this shit," said Nina as she looked at Tamika, knowing she was crazy.

"What you gonna do, Nina, pay or play? I ain't got all night," lisped a fat man who was playing against her.

"I'ma play, damn. You see my partna ho'n in this motherfucker, damn."

"I can play," Dutch stood behind her partner's chair and said with a smile.

"Huh?"

"I said, I can play till your partner gets back."

She looked him up and down disapprovingly and frowned. *Who he think he is, with his fine ass?* she couldn't help but ask herself.

"You can play?" she asked, but was really asking, *Nigga, who the fuck is you?*

He cocked his head to one side and gave her a "duh" expression. Dutch hadn't played spades since he was locked up for stealing cars eight years ago.

"All right, come on," she said, and Dutch sat down.

At first, because of the dim light, Dutch couldn't really see her. But after he sat down under the hanging overhead lamp he saw her face. He was in love, just like that. Nina had him and hadn't done a thing.

The fat man looked up to see who he was about to open up his can of whoop-ass on.

"Dutch!" the fat man exclaimed, surprised to see Dutch, especially sitting next to him at the same table. *Awwwww, mannn, damnnn,* the fat man thought to himself.

"I got five and a possible," she told Dutch, who for the first time could not maintain his composure. He simply could not do anything but stare at her and wonder if she was as wonderful as she appeared.

The fat dude trembled. What was he to do? Let Dutch win and lose five hundred dollars? Or win five hundred dollars and lose something immensely more valuable? With Dutch, there was just no telling. *What should I bid? Just go board, right? Damn, what the fuck should I do?*

"How many you got?" Nina asked Dutch.

"Huh?" he asked, not thinking about books.

"Is you deaf or something?" she questioned, now pretending to be speaking to a deaf mute, making sign language and talking slowly to him as if he were deaf. "How . . . many . . . do . . . you . . . have?"

The fat man's eyes shot over at Dutch. *Is this bitch crazy? Don't she know who the fuck she clownin'? She must not know this nigga will kill us all,* he kept thinking to himself.

"Oh, damn, my fault. I got two," Dutch said, still not taking his eyes, or his smile, off her.

"Give us eight," said Nina turning to the fat man. He looked at her and wrote down an eight for them and a five for himself and his partner. The lead was on the fat man's partner, who played a four of hearts. Dutch followed suit with a ten, the fat man played a queen, and Nina took the book with an ace.

She then brought hearts back to the board and Dutch won the book with his king. He then played a low diamond to the board.

"Fuck is this dumb muhfucka doin'?" Nina said, almost having a fit. She rumbled under her breath loud enough to be heard.

Just my damn luck, hafta play this nigga and a crazy bitch! She gonna get us both shot the fuck up, the fat man thought as he looked up, hoping that Dutch didn't hear what the crazy girl said.

The hand played out and Dutch and Nina ended up being set with seven.

"Didn't you see me play back hearts? I thought you said you could play?" she huffed at him while she shuffled the cards.

"My fault," Dutch replied in a monotone.

"Mmm-hmm," she mumbled, and rolled her eyes at him.

The game played out and Nina ended up losing. The fat man's partner collected the money as the fat man watched Dutch. Dutch watched Nina get up from the table but didn't say a word.

"How much she lose?" Dutch questioned the fat man.

There it is, now the nigga gonna take my shit, the fat guy thought, but softly responded, "Five hundred."

To his surprise and relief, Dutch got up and walked away in Nina's direction and the fat man's asshole loosened.

Nina was furious as she scanned the crowd for her partner. She finally spotted her.

"Tamika! Tamika!" she shouted, "You ain't shit!"

Tamika turned around, quite tipsy, to see her best friend staring at her. She burst out in laughter.

"You look so funny when you mad," she said as she threw her hand on Nina's shoulder.

"Get off me, man. I lost my fuckin' money. Fuckin' wit' you, I got stuck playin' wit' some dumb motherfucker and you over here tryin' to trick niggas."

"Oh, sour puss! Live a little, bitch, you need to mingle, Ms. Single."

"Um, unlike you, I don't work on my back. I gotta get up in the mornin'," Nina said with a flaccid smile.

"Oh, fuck you, Nina," said her friend with a smile. "Let me tell Derrick I'm leaving. I'll meet you outside, okay, shmuckums?" she said, pinching Nina's cheek.

"You better bring your drunk ass on, nigga, before you be left out here, and you giving me my two-hundred and fifty dollars back off that five I lost," she said as Tamika agreed with her.

Dutch searched the crowd and spotted Nina heading out

the door. He bumped into people in the crowded after-hours spot as he rushed to her.

"Nina!" he called out. She turned around to see who was calling.

When she saw Dutch, she sucked her teeth, pursed her lips, and kept on walking.

"It's like that?" Dutch asked, not believing she could be that rude.

"Hell, yeah! Just like that, nigga, make me lose my money," she said over her shoulder.

"I'm sayin', I'm trying to give you something, if you'd just stop," he said, really hoping she would.

Nina slowed her stroll, then spun around on her stilettoes and folded her arms across her chest, "What?"

"A girl will listen if she thinks you got something for her?" he asked, hoping her character wasn't like that at all. "You left this," he said, holding five hundred-dollar bills.

She looked at the money in his hand. "And what's that suppose to be?"

"Your money. That's how much you bet, ain't it?"

"Yeah, but that ain't my five hundred dollars, 'cause I lost my five hundred dollars fuckin' around wit' you. You made sure I lost."

"Yeah, well, that's why I'm givin' you this. I sorta lied to you when I said I knew how to play," Dutch admitted.

"Noaa, ya think? I woulda never guessed. Good-bye."

Nina turned and walked away. She spotted Tamika.

"Dutch?" Tamika questioned. She was looking at the jackpot, and couldn't believe it. "Hi, Dutch," Tamika sang to him.

Dutch recognized the girl as someone Craze ran through,

or maybe it was Zoom he had seen with the broad. He nodded in response, but kept his attention on Nina.

"Okay, at least let me take you to a late dinner," Dutch
offered.

"No."

"Call it an early breakfast then."

"Was it the N or the O, that you didn't get?" Nina questioned smartly, although her attitude didn't show it. She
liked his determination and the fact that he came clean and
was truthful about the spade game. She also liked that he
had offered to repay her loss.

"Well, can I—" Dutch stammered before Nina cut
him off.

"Good night," she said sternly, looking in his baby browns,
honestly wishing she hadn't said it. Yet she turned and
walked away.

Tamika was beside herself. *The girl is crazy! I knew she
needed help, but damn!* Tamika thought after witnessing her
best friend turn down the most desirable and wanted man
in town.

"Girl, do you know who that was? Dutch!"

"And I'm 'posed to get naked right there and start fuckin'
the nigga or something?"

"Shit, bitch, if you knew what the fuck I know, you'd be
doin' something," Tamika said, knowing Nina knew better.

"Girl, you need counseling," joked Nina as she unlocked
the car door.

"No, you do. I got a ride. My Puerto Rican friend wants
to go to breakfast," Tamika said, grinning from ear to ear.
"So I wrote down his tag number. Give it to the police, if you

never hear from me again," she said seriously as she passed a piece of paper with the stranger's tag number written on it.

"Yeah, bitch, counseling," hollered Nina as she waved good night with the piece of paper in her hand.

Four days later, it was pouring rain. Nina's car broke down on her way to work, so she was forced to take a cab home. She hated Newark cabs and disliked the trip all the way home to Elizabeth. But she especially hated taking the bus. Nina stood on her feet all day at the bank dealing with rude, dumb, slow, deaf, and crazy people. After work, she didn't have the tolerance for a crowded, stuffy, smelly bus ride. If it weren't for her living expenses, she would have spent every day doing what she enjoyed most: sleeping.

After eating Chinese food leftovers, she took a relaxing, long, hot bubble bath. Sleeping was exactly what she intended to do. She hit the remote to the stereo system and her speakers filled her small apartment with Nina Simone, whom her mother had named her after.

The answering machine blinked with messages, but she didn't want to hear them. There would possibly be a call from a bill collector and probably a call from Tamika bragging about something. A man with jewels and money or something somebody had bought her. Maybe there would be a message from her mother, asking her usual questions. And she especially did not want to hear her ex-boyfriend's sorry attempts to resume the relationship, which had been over for more than a month and a half.

All of a sudden, the phone rang, disrupting Nina Simone's melody and Nina's train of thought.

"Go away," she said to the ringing phone.

She took another bite of her chicken lo mein and finally answered it.

"Hello?"

"Hello, is this Nina?" asked an unfamiliar man's voice.

"Depends on who wants to know," she said, truly curious about who it could be.

The voice laughed smoothly and she connected it to a smile she couldn't forget . . .

Dutch.

"May I ask how you got this number?"

"Your friend, Tamika."

"And may I ask if I didn't give it to you, what made you think I wanted you to have it?"

"Women are funny like that. They say yes when they mean no and say no when they mean yes," Dutch philosophized.

"Oh, really? That's the same bullshit that got Mike Tyson's ass all fucked up," she quipped.

"Exactly, if that broad did say no, she meant yes," said Dutch, on his man Mike's side. "So, um, is that Nina Simone I hear playing?"

"It's Nina," she confirmed, before adding, "Listen . . . Dutch, is it?"

"Bernard James, but don't let that out," he said, smiling to himself, having waited days to hear her voice again.

"How'd you get a name like Dutch, anyway?" She digressed, out of curiosity, from what she had intended to say.

"Maybe I'll tell you tonight over dinner."

"Listen, Bernard, you seem like . . . like a cool cat to get to know. You know, you are real handsome and to be honest, I dig your style, but it's just . . . that . . . I don't know.

I just got out of this corny relationship and well . . . it's the timing," she fought for the words, trying to be polite and not state the real reason.

"Okay, then, I'll call you tomorrow and you just think about what you want to say," said Dutch, needing to dial her phone tomorrow.

"No, really, I'm serious, Dutch," she said, wishing she didn't have to be.

"So is this good-bye?" Dutch questioned.

"I guess it is," she said, hanging up the phone.

For the next few days, Dutch crossed her mind a million times. She liked him, his style, his look, his class, but like Dutch, she too had rules, which also, like Dutch, she never broke. She didn't deal with hustlers. It wasn't a question of being a saint or a sinner, but she did have her reasons.

Four years before, when her family lived in Pioneer Homes housing projects in Elizabeth, her younger brother had been killed. He was only sixteen, two years younger than her at the time. He had been hustling for Bilal Petelow. Bilal had Elizabeth on lock, when it came to the coke game.

She had been dating Lover J, one of Bilal's main men. She and Lover J were in the parking lot arguing about a girl she heard he was creeping with when she heard a series of gunshots. The shots seemed to last forever, but in reality ended after a few seconds. Lover J was about to pull out of the lot when Nina heard her mother's screams.

She jumped out of the car, ran into the courtyard, and saw her mother cradling her dead brother. Her mother's nightgown was drenched in his blood. The sight of her dead brother brought the reality of the game too close to home that night, and she swore she would distance herself. She

didn't want to change the world or become a social worker.
She just wanted to learn from her brother's mistake, respect
his memory, and get on with her life.

But thoughts of Dutch were now making that difficult
to do.

Two days later, Dutch was standing in her line at the
bank, carrying a large burlap sack.

"Hello." He smiled to her.

"Hi," she said, standing on her tippy toes and peering
over the counter.

"What's in the b—" she began to ask before he cut her off.

"Never mind that. Have I sent you flowers?"

"No," she said, confused.

"What about diamonds to your doorstep?"

"No, but," she said with her usual disposition, attempting
to shut him down.

"Will you let me finish? I been practicin' this shit all day,"
he said, as a blushing Nina smiled and let him continue.

"Thank you. Now, being that I coulda' easily did those
things and more, why do you think I haven't?"

She just looked at him, not answering.

"Because! Some things are priceless, because no one will
pay for them, while others are priceless, because no one can
pay for them," he said, smiling like he knew something no
one else did.

"And?" she asked, questioning relevancy.

"And all I'm asking is a chance to sit down with you. No
barriers, no phones, no cards, and either you let me convince
you of my sincerity or let me get you out my system," he
said. He had been unable to eat or sleep over Nina.

"And if I refuse?"

"Then that's what the bag is for. This gots to be at least two thousand dollars in pennies and I will be needing 'em wrapped and counted."

"Oh, an ultimatum? Well, did you consider before you drug that bag in here that you need an account with us for that service?"

"I just opened one."

She smiled back before answering. "If I do sit down with you, it will be on my terms."

"Okay," answered Dutch. His heart lightened and he could breathe again.

"My time, my date, my choice, my way."

"I personally wouldn't have it any other way."

She stood back and appraised the ebony prince before her. *Who are you and why do I care to know?*

It was true, Dutch had Nina at hello. She just didn't know it yet.

"How you?" Dutch asked as he leaned on her door frame four days later. He brought with him a fistful of flowers and his trademark smile.

"I'm fine," she said, letting him in.

She didn't want to go out with a hustler only to meet the same fate her brother did, by association. Instead, she invited him over for dinner. She prepared a simple chicken and vegetable casserole. It was nothing fancy, but delicious. The evening was friendly, without too much familiarity, though they flirted with each other.

"Look at your smile. You can't tell me the ladies don't melt right out their panties."

"Melt?" he said, questioning her choice of words, even though he knew she wasn't wrong.

If rhythm could be judged like an Olympic event, Dutch would score a ten, a true dime. He was totally different from all the men she had ever dated. They tried to buy her affections and to pressure her into giving them away. Dutch continued to surprise her. Not only was he wealthy, he was articulate and intelligent, exuding confidence (which she loved), and was so, so fine. "Quenching, like a tall glass of water on a hot sunny day," her grandmother used to say.

She found herself over the next few weeks slipping into a too-comfortable comfort zone, something she hadn't planned to do, something she couldn't help but do. She was drawn to Dutch from the moment he asked her could he play her card game. It was as if he had cast a spell on her. Nina didn't want to let go. The more time she spent with him, the more she wanted to see him, to touch him, to be next to him.

Between his business trips to France, running the streets, taking care of all his businesses, and everything else, Dutch spent all his spare time getting to know Nina. He had gathered a lot about her over several months, knowing where she worked and lived and traveled in her daily routine. He remembered everything she said as if his memory was a recorder. He listened to her when she talked about problems and offered her strong, sound advice, usually street advice, pumping her up to meet whatever challenge she faced. He believed in her more than she believed in herself, and that was the only weakness in her that he had found.

He sent her flowers and imported sweet chocolate; he always brought a bottle of wine when he went to her and often asked if she needed anything. He was always ready to shower

her with whatever she wanted or needed. Her response, however, was always a stern, flat "No" or "I'm fine."

Dutch loved her independence. And he was glad she had
her bank job. However, Nina used it against him and would
not give in. The average broad, dead brother or not, would
be rolling with him and he knew it. He still hadn't had sex
with her after four months. And while he wasn't pressed, he
wanted to say that they were more than friends.

Dutch knew what he wanted. He wanted Nina to be his
wife. He wanted to wake up looking at her face every morning
and go to sleep with her by his side. He had never believed
he could feel so strongly about a person. His actions expressed
only love for her, and she had to feel it, she had to know.

Dinner at her place came around again and Dutch finally
had his chance to make a move on Nina. They were sitting
on the couch, laughing at something she said. She slapped
his leg and he gently placed his hand on top of hers. Holding her hand, he looked in her eyes. He reached for the back
of her head and slowly kissed her lips, exploring everything
there was to explore as she gently sucked his tongue. He
felt his dick harden as he swirled his tongue in and out of
her mouth. Moving his body toward her, his hands slowly
slid from the nape of her neck down her back to her ass. He
palmed her butt and thighs and sucked the skin of her neck.
As he pushed her back against the cushions he pulled at her
bra and reached between her legs.

"Stop, Dutch. No," she said, pushing him away and standing up to adjust her clothes and ponytail.

"Wha?" Dutch couldn't believe it.

"I . . . I can't. I'm just . . . I can't."

"Listen, I respect everything about you, ma. If you don't

want to, I understand. I'll wait my life for you. You hear me?" Dutch pleaded for her to understand.

He knew other men made false promises of "I love you" to get into a woman's panties, but it wasn't his reality to say anything to get what he wanted.

"Why are you here? What do you want from me?" Nina asked, looking confused and unsure.

"I don't know. Why are you here?" he asked back, looking at her seriously.

"I live here."

"Well, I was invited over."

"Maybe you just refuse to leave me alone because your male ego can't handle the fact that there's something in this world that you can't have."

Dutch looked at her and didn't say anything. But his eyes told her that she was wrong.

"Come on, Dutch, admit it. How many women have you gone after that you didn't get? And you know they say we always want what we can't have."

"Nina, let me let you in on something. Correction number one, you are the first woman I've ever gone after in my life, and that's word to my moms, B. And correction number two, I don't want you. I'm trying to figure out what is so special about you that's worth me wanting in the first place. Shit, that's what I'm startin' to think."

"Well, excuse me."

"And, if I did want you, why would you be what I can't have? Why?"

He asked the one question that was at the core of their relationship

"Because I'm not a possession," Nina said.

"Then what are you? Possessive?" asked Dutch, hitting the nail on the head and seeing it in Nina's response as they both laughed.

"You know, they say possessive people are insecure!" he said, hitting another nail on the head.

"Let's take a walk. I want to show you something," she said, truly at a loss for words.

Her apartment wasn't far from where she had grown up in Pioneer Homes. They walked to the projects' outer courtyard, where she pointed to a wall.

It was dark but Dutch could see a mural on it. He made out the name "Trick" in big, bold, capital letters. And he could see the image of a young black boy's face with the initials RIP underneath.

"That was my brother. He was killed four years ago right in front of our apartment."

"Drugs?" he asked as he looked at the wall again and understood her pain.

"I didn't want you to think what I'm feelin' is you or got anything to do with you. I had fun with you these past few months. I actually have the best times when I'm with you. I like you, Dutch . . . I really do. I don't want you to think I'm not feeling your person. You are so smooth and so handsome. It's just that, he was my blood," she said as a tear dropped down the side of her face. It was a little tear for both her brother and for Dutch, whom she had to let go.

"You think I'll end up like him, that you'll lose me, too?" asked Dutch.

"No, not that," she said, looking in his eyes as if it were much worse. "No, people die in traffic accidents on their way to church. So, it's not the loss, it's the respect. The respect I have for my brother's life, for his memory. I can't see myself living off what he died for. I can't be a part of it."

"So, if your brother died in a car accident, would that mean you would never ride in a car again?" he asked as she looked away.

There wasn't much for Dutch to say. His heart was shattered by her words and crushed by her silence. He respected her values, her conviction, and her loyalty to her brother. She had made it clear that she had her world and he had his, and there would be no mixing of the two. Like Dutch, she too had rules, and while she strained, she never bent.

"Nina, you ever heard the saying, when you love something, set it free? If it is meant to be, it'll come back to you?"

She shook her head yes as she looked into his eyes.

"Then I'll say no more and I'll leave you alone."

They were exactly the same in opposite ways, which made their situation bittersweet. Nina didn't say anything. She just looked at Dutch with sad tears in her eyes for her brother. But she wouldn't bend, not even for Dutch.

He had slipped, but it was the sweetest mistake he had ever made. Looking at the mural one more time, he shook his head. *This all your fault, you know that, right?* he asked, hoping one day, maybe, that Nina would change her mind.

CHAPTER ELEVEN

◆

CROOKED

Detective David O'Neal," said the one-eyed white man sitting on the stand, identifying himself before the court.

The man on the stand looked normal. Except for the black patch over his right eye. Jacobs had made sure, however, that O'Neal made a grand entrance in his wheelchair. He had no legs.

Michael Glass pinched the bridge of his nose with his index finger and thumb as O'Neal rolled by. The jury uncomfortably watched as he climbed onto the witness stand with exacerbated labor.

Dutch found it ironic that O'Neal had lost his legs. The old man had never stood on his own anyway. He was like a leech, and Dutch regretted that the blast hadn't killed him. Now here he was to testify.

"And how long have you been on the police force, Detective?"

"Twenty-three years, but I'm retired now," O'Neal answered.

"Can I ask why? Was it age?"

"I'll tell you why! 'Cause of that sonofabitch over there!" O'Neal roared as the judge banged his gavel.

"Counselor, please control your witness."

"I'm sorry, Your Honor, I really am. But how would you feel if one day you wake up, kiss your wife, and go to work and before you've finished your morning coffee, your whole body is being ripped apart and you wake up like this?" O'Neal asked, gesturing to his nonexistent legs.

"I understand, sir, and I empathize with you, but this is a court of law," advised the judge, feeling pity and sadness for the fallen police detective.

"I understand, Your Honor."

Jacobs allowed a moment to pass so O'Neal could adjust himself, then began again.

"Now, Mr. O'Neal, you claim Bernard James is the cause of your early retirement?"

"Yes, he ordered that the Twenty-ninth Precinct be blown up. He had a psycho walk into the station, strapped with C-4. He blew up himself and my fellow officers," claimed O'Neal as he fought back his tears, remembering the horrific afternoon.

"Now, Mr. O'Neal, how can you be sure that it was Bernard James who was responsible for the explosion on November 11, 1998?" asked Jacobs.

"The suicide bomber was named William Brent. He also went by the name Bill Blass. He was a small-time hustler. I had known him for quite some time. Apparently mailed his wife a letter prior to entering the station that morning," O'Neal explained.

Jacobs walked over to his table and returned with an envelope and a sheet of paper.

"Is this the letter to Mrs. Brent postmarked November 11, 1998?"

"Yes, that is the letter," said O'Neal as he inspected it.

"And would you read the letter to the court, please."

"Objection, Your Honor!" Glass bellowed as he stood from his desk. "Defense has never received a copy of this letter during discovery, Your Honor."

"Your Honor, the letter was obtained by my office from Lieutenant Service of the Twenty-ninth Precinct two weeks ago. It was too late to admit the letter into discovery," Jacobs explained.

"Overruled. You may proceed, but this letter better be taking us somewhere relevant, Mr. Jacobs," Judge Whitaker said, allowing the testimony to proceed.

O'Neal looked at the letter and then looked at the jury. He fixed himself to be more comfortable then began to read.

"Dear Monique, by the time you get this, I'll be dead, but I wanted you to know that it's because of Dutch. He said if I don't do what he say, he gonna kill you, the kids, and my whole family. So, this is my sacrifice. I gladly make it, too. All I ask is that if you get this letter, you deliver it to the proper authorities, the DA or somebody like that. Don't give it to no regular cop, though. I love you, pray for my soul. Love Always, Billy," O'Neal concluded, then looked up. Jacobs took the letter from him, thanking him for reading it to the court.

"Your Honor, the state moves to introduce this letter as State Exhibit J-43," said Jacobs, with the case all figured out.

Michael Glass stood up and exclaimed, "Objection, Your Honor, the letter did not once mention my client's name, and secondly, that letter doesn't give a clear portrait of him being instructed by anybody to blow up a police precinct."

"It said Dutch! Everybody knows who Dutch is!" O'Neal blurted out.

The judge banged his gavel and looked over at the witness.

"Mr. O'Neal, I'm not going to warn you again. Strike the last comment."

"Your Honor, I believe it has been established beyond a reasonable doubt that Bernard James is in fact known by the moniker Dutch."

"No, we may have established Bernard James as a Dutch, but we cannot say beyond a reasonable doubt that Bernard James is the only Dutch in the city. How many people could there be with the same nickname?" asked Glass, looking confused over the subject matter.

"May I see the letter, please?" asked the judge.

He took the letter and decided he wanted to eat the slice of banana cream pie his wife had sent with his bagged lunch.

"Court will take a ten-minute recess while I review this letter in my chambers."

He banged his gavel as Dutch thought of Bill. His name used to ring bells everywhere. He had longevity, which gave him a respected notch on the urban ladder. He had seen the rise and fall of many a young hustler, so Dutch respected Bill Blass for his expertise and street-savvy wisdom, even though he was not a major player.

Angel had walked into Dutch's used-car lot on Elizabeth Avenue to find Dutch and Craze playfully arguing while they sat in an '84 Volvo.

"Man, you ain't never stole no Accord wit' out poppin' the neck, lyin' muhfucker." Dutch laughed.

"Nigga, fuck you," Craze retorted.

"Y'all still two little kids," Angel said, leaning into the car.

"Yo, tell this dumb-ass nigga, you gotta pop the neck on Accords," Dutch instructed Angel.

"Fuck that, listen, I got somebody in the car wantin' to talk to you."

"Who?"

"Bill Blass," Angel responded.

Dutch looked at his watch. "What he want?"

"A job."

Dutch looked at Craze, then slowly got out the car. He approached Angel's droptop Lexus. Bill was sitting in the passenger seat smoking a cigarette. Dutch shook his hand, leaning on the door.

"What up, Bill?"

"You, baby. Of course, I ain't gotta tell you that," he said as Dutch chuckled. "Yo, I'm hurtin'. It's hard down my end in J.C. Them young bucks forgettin' who put the G in this here game, Duke."

"And?" asked Dutch.

"And," Bill responded as if to say, you know what I want.

Dutch knew Bill had a good reputation for putting in work, but Blass was also known for taking long addiction sabbaticals. If he hadn't had a crack monkey riding around on his back, he would have been rich a long time ago. He could get the loot, though. Problem was what he did after he got it. Dutch knew both sides of Bill's rep and he knew Blass knew his.

"Who he fuck wit'?" he asked Angel.

"Blitz from Bergen," she answered.

They both knew Blitz was on the run from the feds.

"You in luck, B, my man Blitz on vacation," said Dutch, and just like that, Bill Blass found himself a lieutenant in Jersey City.

For seven straight months Bill Blass operated like the vet Dutch respected him for being. Bill handled his business like a champ. He had Dutch's money on time. He had the spots in check, and he was available at Dutch's beck and call.

But then word got around that he had started smoking crack again. Dutch told Roc to keep a close eye on him, even though Roc stressed to him to fire Blass.

"Man, that nigga smokin', man. I'm tellin' you the other crackheads be knowing some shit. Somebody said he was in the bodega buying boxes of matches," said Roc.

"Roc, stop trickin' crackheads. I'ma call Ayesha," Dutch said jokingly, but at the same time he knew what Roc said needed to be investigated.

It was a Tuesday at three-fifteen in the morning when Roberto called Dutch.

"Uh, Dutch, I don't know how to tell you this. Fat Tony died in a car accident last night."

"Wha' you say?" Dutch asked Roberto as he gave him the horrible news.

"We don't know nothing yet, just that he's gone," said Roberto as Dutch solemnly stood at the window, watching the moving traffic.

Dutch was a part of Fat Tony's funeral service. He was, and had always been, Tony's guy. Everyone knew Dutch was the black kid that Tony had taken under his wing. It was also at Fat Tony's service that Dutch started to understand.

"Now that Tony's dead, I guess you'll be retiring, huh?" Frankie Bonno asked with a smirk on his face.

Dutch's heart ached for the old guy, but he got the gist of Frankie's question. Dutch knew in his heart of hearts that Fat Tony's death was no accident.

"Why would I, when I inherit what me and Fat Tony built?"

These words from Dutch boiled Frankie's blood. *Who the fuck does this nigger think he is? I'ma show him.* And it was then and there in DiQuallo's Funeral Home that a war began. Dutch just didn't know it had been declared. But he would soon enough.

After the services, Dutch flew to France for business, consumed by the loss of a man he dearly loved and respected— Fat Tony, his mentor. He had learned the politics, as well as the streets, from the man. Fat Tony and the entire Cerone family backed politicians like horses based on their ability to run . . . and win. Thanks to Fat Tony's influence and the strong arm of his army, the Zoo Crew, who were fast becoming legends themselves, Newark had a new mayor and his name was Dutch. Nothing would ever change that. Frankie Bonno could try, but Dutch would die before he let him take what he had built. The forces that be, however, would change his destiny.

Slowly.

In less than ninety days after Frankie Bonno made a

phone call, Dutch's entire world began to crumble, just like
that. His neighborhood nightspots were raided, one after the
other, night after night. No one wanted to go to a spot if the
police were coming in after them, and the police were coming. The cost to Dutch was considerable.

His street team, the Zoo Crew, was getting knocked so
often that there was no one left to hustle on street corners.
If they opened a spot, it was raided and shut down as fast as
it was opened.

Then, just when Dutch thought things could get no
worse and his luck was about to change, he got a phone call
from Roc.

"Yo, Duke, I don't know how to tell you this, man," he
said, nervously. "That nigga Blass missing and so is the coke
and the heroin out both houses. The shit is gone and he done
drilled the entire safe up out the floor, man. It's . . . it's gone,
Dutch."

Roc did not know how Dutch would handle the news,
and that was why he told him over the phone. *Fuck tellin' that
crazy muhfucka in person,* Roc thought.

Dutch, however, couldn't think. His mind raced. Close to
$875,000 worth of money and drugs was gone.

Gone.

He started sweating as he thought of how to get his
money back. He needed it right now. Half his army was
in jail, and the cops confiscated more of his money every
time they raided one of his nightspots. So far, they had
taken close to $470,00 in cash and $150,000 worth of
drugs.

Dutch was getting more money than the Italians thought
he should have been allowed to get. That's what it boiled

down to. Had he been Italian, Fat Tony's wishes would have been respected in death. But Dutch wasn't Italian. He was a nigger. Frankie Bonno had permission and the police were on his payroll. Dutch was screwed.

All the money he had made before Fat Tony died was enough to pay his army and the mob. Everything was fine until Fat Tony died and Frankie Bonno decided it was time to collect what should have been his all along. The other families agreed. It was the Italian way, and Dutch was up shit creek with no paddle.

Fat Tony, Bill Blass, his missing money, his missing coke, his missing heroin, Frankie Bonno, his army locked down, as if on D-block with Jada, and no Nina. The ball was dropping, fast, yet the only thought spinning in his mind . . . *Where is Bill Blass?*

After Dutch put out a bounty on his head, it only took two weeks to find him. Bill Blass was hiding out in Ohio. One of Angel's Charlies got a call from a cat named Jesus from Brooklyn. Jesus was in Cleveland putting in work and spotted Blass in a bar, buying out the motherfucker.

Dutch sent two Charlies with a bag of "thank-you" money for Jesus, and the Charlies brought Bill Blass back to Newark tied up in the trunk of a Lincoln Town Car.

When Dutch finally saw Bill, the Charlies had him tied, naked, to a chair in a small room at the Irvington Motor Lodge. Bill begged for his life through duct tape taped over his mouth. Dutch sat on the bed and looked at him eye level while ripping the tape from his mouth.

"My man Bill Blass. I'm sayin' you gonna just leave and not even say good-bye, after all I did for you?"

The two Charlies who had retrieved Bill from Ohio stood

on both sides of him with guns drawn to his head, even though he was tied up.

"Listen, Dutch, whatever you thinkin', man, it ain't like that. I swear. I mean, you seen how shit was gettin' in J.C. It was on fire, so I just went to lay low for a minute, my word. I was bringing the money and your shit back. I only took it in case of a raid, so it wouldn't get lost," said Bill as he felt Dutch remove the diamond bezel Presidential Rolex from his wrist, which was tied behind him.

"All the way to Ohio, Duke? I mean, damn, Roc said the safe all out the floor and you protecting me from the law. That shit make you look fucked up, Blass, especially since you holdin' my fuckin' paper."

Dutch had retrieved a little over six hundred thousand dollars when Blass was captured, and he also took possession of a brand-new Range Rover Blass had bought. The Rolex watch was his now, too.

"Naw, Dutch, I'm your man, an—"

"That shit you sayin' ain't important right now. What's important is that you here now and I got some of my fuckin' paper back. We'll talk about my coke and dope later. What's important is that I need you to do something for me and only you can handle this shit for me, Blass."

Blass was relieved to hear Dutch's tone. He just knew Dutch was buying into the story. All he wanted was to be untied so he could put his clothes back on.

"Do you think I can get dressed, first?" asked Blass.

"Naw, nigga, hold up."

"Dutch, whatever you need me for, man, you don't have to worry. I got you. I'm your man," Blass said with assurance. Dutch cocked his head to the side.

"Oh, yeah?" he said as he nodded to one of the Charlies. The girl went into the bathroom and came back out with a suitcase. She placed it on the bed next to Dutch and popped the lid to reveal a strange vest with blocks of what looked like clay attached. Blass refocused, saw the wires, and realized the blocks weren't clay. They were C-4 explosives.

"Wha . . . what's that for?" he whispered meekly, not fully understanding but knowing deep down that what he had done would cost him his life.

"What's that for? Nigga, that's the option vest! Option one, I kill your wife, your kids, your mother, your father, your grandfather, your cousin in West Bubblefuck workin' in that fuckin' supermarket to save money, whoever, wherever. If I find a nigga with your last name, I'm murderin' they asses, from babies to their late eighties, you hear me, nigga? Your whole fuckin, family. You think I'm playin'? You ever known me to play, nigga?"

Blass slowly shook his head.

"And option two is you strap on that vest right there and walk into the police station offa Bergen during the morning shift and detonate yourself."

Dutch sat back and waited for Bill's response. All Bill could think of was his family. The life he had led had put him in this position and he cursed himself for allowing anyone to have power over him. *Who the hell does he think he is threatening me like this?* Blass thought to himself. But Dutch had spoken and Bill knew he was a dead man. He didn't even need an afterthought.

Yet, as a hustler, Blass knew the hearts of men. He could pick a young wolf out of the pack and would know if the kid would last a year in the game. He had watched Dutch come up since the nigga had been stealing cars and always saw the potential in young Dutch. He also knew Dutch was far from playing games. Chances were that the motherfuckers were parked outside his house this very moment waiting for a call from Dutch.

"Why me?"

"Nigga, why you? Why not you, muhfucka? Why you? Like you didn't drill my safe out the floor and take my fucking money and my fucking coke. Nigga, is you fuckin' crazy? Nigga got a brand-new Range Rover and Rolex and he gonna ask me, why him?" Dutch asked, looking at one of the Charlies before looking back at Blass.

"Muhfucker, that wasn't you in Ohio buying out the bar with my fuckin' money? Nigga, shut the fuck up before option three is no option and I just start cutting off your kids' heads while you watch, pussy."

The tears streaked down Bill's cheeks as he agreed to commit suicide in the name of Dutch and in order to save his family.

Dutch returned to the present, to O'Neal on the witness stand. The former detective was describing the events of the day when Bill Blass walked into the police precinct and detonated himself.

Dutch wondered what Blass was thinking before he detonated himself. *Probably wished he had left my money and my coke the fuck alone,* thought Dutch as O'Neal continued to dramatize the incident.

O'Neal then pulled out a list of the fallen heroes and called their names, so the jury would know who had died.

This nigga got some nerve, thought Dutch. *Tell 'em about yourself and how you was on the payroll for the mob all your life. Tell 'em how you had no honor or loyalty to a muhfucka that was feeding you. Tell 'em that's why you ain't got no legs.*

Dutch remembered his last conversation with O'Neal. It was at Eleganza, a strip bar on Sixteenth Avenue. As usual, he was drunk and partying with his usual stripper girl up on the stage. He had been there for over an hour, consuming much beer and liquor. His full bladder had forced him to make his way to the men's room.

O'Neal staggered in and found it empty. He was humming a Donna Summer tune to the thumping bass that vibrated the bathroom walls. He was unzipping his pants at the urinal when he heard the door open. He paid no attention until he felt his collar yanked up, jerking his body to the floor. He was dragged to an empty stall.

It all happened so fast. He suddenly found himself on the floor of the stall with his head between the partition and the commode, his pants still unzipped, his penis dangling out of the slit in his zipper.

"Fucked-up way to die, with your dick in your hand."

He looked up at Dutch, groggily, with blurred vision. Craze stood over him. Both men held guns pointed at him.

"Wha-what the fuck do you think you're doing?" he slurred, still dazed from his fall. He tried to get up, but Dutch punched him in the face, hard, sending him back between the wall and the commode. He put his gun to O'Neal's face and clicked the clip, loading his weapon.

"So, after all these years, this is how you do me, muhfucker, huh?" asked Dutch.

"Wait a minute," O'Neal hollered, realizing the gravity of the situation.

"Nigga, you ain't got a minute! You think I don't know what you doin'?! You raided all my spots and my teams gettin' bagged and you think I don't know what's going on?"

"Okay, okay! You want the fuckin' truth! It's over for you, Dutch, and I'll be damned if I'm going down with you! Fat Tony is dead and I'm going with Frank!"

Dutch gripped the gun tighter, on the verge of pulling the trigger, and O'Neal felt it. He saw his life flash before him.

"Oh, you think just 'cause Tony dead you can roll over on me? Nigga, I'm Dutch, you fuckin' sellout. Fuck Tony, fuck Frank, and fuck you! I'm Dutch. Nigga, I say when it's over."

O'Neal could see the cold, bitter hatred in Dutch's eyes, but he was determined to meet his death like a man.

"Then go 'head, kill me. Go 'head, but it ain't gonna change nothing. Everybody's goin' wit' Frank. So what, you kill me, won't change nothing. You might as well kill us all 'cause nobody's on your side no more," said O'Neal in a drunken stupor, yet speaking the truth.

The alcohol made him braver than he would normally have been.

"Yeah, I might as well," said Dutch, deciding to take O'Neal up on his offer. But then he turned and walked out of the bathroom with Craze behind him, keeping an eye on O'Neal.

"You was Dutch! You nobody now. You hear me? Nobody, nigga!" O'Neal said, laughing, until he glanced down at his uncovered genitals and realized he'd pissed on himself.

"Shit!"

The story he told the jury was pretty much the same, except for peeing on himself. When he finished he looked directly at Dutch. *Betcha' wish you'd killed me, don't cha, motherfucker?* O'Neal thought but said with his eyes. Dutch nodded to him as if reading his mind.

Jacobs walked back to his table, but before he sat down, he had one more question.

"Mr. O'Neal, you've been on the force for twenty-three years, decorated several times in uniform, and you are a highly respected member of the police force. So, I ask you, why would you sacrifice your reputation after all these years when you have nothing to gain and literally everything to lose?"

"I know my dealings with the Cerone family were wrong. However, this man murdered twenty-eight officers to send a message to only a few. I'd sacrifice my life to bring him to justice," said O'Neal with honesty and sincerity.

"I have no more questions, Your Honor," said Jacobs with a smile on his face.

Dutch watched as O'Neal climbed back into his wheel-chair. He definitely regretted not killing O'Neal when he had the chance. *Yeah, I should have killed him when I had the chance,* Dutch agreed to himself.

Frankie Bonno was playing dirty, applying pressure, waiting for Dutch to break. Dutch thought of Fat Tony's death. He thought of how everything had changed, as a result of that one man no longer breathing. He had enemies now, and he knew they meant business.

Frankie Sorbonno had it all figured out: how Dutch would go to jail, how the streets of Newark would be his, and how he would take back what he believed to be his.

And while Frankie had it all mapped up, he neglected to notice that Dutch did, too.

.

CHAPTER TWELVE

◆

FRANK'S PLACE

Frank Sorbonno, aka Frankie Bonno, sat in his Sportsman's Club across the street from Fat Tony's Italian Restaurant. Frank was on top of the world. The car accident and death of Fat Tony was a bright sunny day after forty days and forty nights of rain.

It had been a long road for Frank working under Tony for so many years. *And he had the nerve to give my spot to Dutch, a nigger, at that,* was how he felt about it. But in truth, he hadn't always despised Tony. Although he considered him fat, lazy, and dumb, in his heart, Frankie believed the only reason Tony had such a powerful position was his family ties to Nevada. But now that Tony was gone, Frank felt that the throne was finally in its rightful hands . . .

His.

He and his cronies sat around the bar watching a New Jersey Devils hockey game. The mood was light until Frank heard the door and looked over to see Dutch, accompanied by Craze, carrying a briefcase.

Frank stared at Dutch with hatred and disgust. *Who the hell does this guy think he is coming in here?* He thought back

to the night Dutch had walked into Fat Tony's with the garbage bag. Dutch had the same stone-cold look tonight.

One of the bodyguards nearest the door approached
Dutch in an attempt to frisk him, but Dutch eyed him so
coldly it froze him and caused another bodyguard to stand
up with his hand on his gun.

"Hey, hey, calm down. Don't you know who this is?
Dutch, the black Al Capone," Frank sarcastically remarked,
laughing at his joke.

He remembered the garbage bag Dutch had brought
with him that night. He later discovered that it contained
Kazami's head. It humiliated and angered the seasoned
mobster that this little black kid had done so easily what
had twice eluded him. But that was not the extent of his
hatred. It had grown deeper when he learned that Fat Tony
had given Dutch his protection and support. Fat Tony knew
Frankie wanted to take over the drug trade in northern
New Jersey.

So, here was Dutch, and he knew that Dutch had come
to ask for mercy . . .

But Frank had other plans.

"Come on in, Dutchie," said Frank.

"You got something against me, Frank?" Dutch asked,
wanting to clear the air.

"Whatever would make you think that?"

"O'Neal."

"You know how it is, Dutchie. You win some, you lose
some, the sun can't shine forever," said Frank as he poured
himself another drink.

Dutch looked at Craze. He knew the game Frank was
trying to play, but he was in no mood to spar. If Frank

wanted a war, he would get one. But the foreplay was about to end.

"So, how long we gonna play this word game?" Dutch asked.

"I got all day," Frank said, shrugging his shoulders and looking at his watch.

Dutch walked over to the table Frank was sitting at and set a briefcase on top of it. He flipped it open to reveal that it was filled with money, a hundred thousand dollars.

"What's that suppose to be?"

"A start."

"You hear this guy? A start," he said, looking at the crony seated nearest to him.

He picked up a stack of money and riffled through it, then pulled out a cigar. He bit off the tip, spat it on the floor, and turned to his crony.

"You got a light?"

The guy handed Frank a lighter. Frank held it up to one of the stacks of money from the briefcase, eyeing Dutch as he put the lighter to the money and watched the stack catch fire. When there was a decent flame burning from the stack, he lit his cigar, fanned out the burning money, and threw it back in the suitcase.

He pointed the cigar at Dutch and said, "Let me tell you something, you stupid black son of a bitch. You know what your problem is? You wanted too much, too fast, too easy. You tried to take what another man earned, then tried to turn around and build your foundation on another man's name. But you forgot the first rule of this shit; you live and die by you and you alone. Sure, you were a little crazier than the rest, a little more ruthless, but you had to be."

Frank stood up and walked around the table. He stood face-to-face with Dutch, even though Dutch was a head taller.

"You thought you were sooo smart, didn't cha? Thought you could say, fuck the rules, and play by your own, huh? I gotta give it to ya, kid. You got balls, but you see, now I got your balls right here in the palm of my hand. Tony can't save you now, so I'm squeezin', and here you come wit' fuckin' candy money and expect a hug and a fuckin' nigger parade! Well, I don't know what you and Tony had going, but I ain't Tony! I'ma keep squeezin' until you squirm, until I get bored with you sufferin', and then I'm gonna crush you like the piss-ass-nigger you are, *capisce?*"

Dutch and Frank locked eyes, and Dutch understood why he was reacting the way he was.

Fear.

Frank feared Dutch. Dutch had finally seen through his facade, to the insecure little man that Frank really was. But he also knew Frankie was a coward behind a brick wall, a dangerous coward behind an almost impenetrable brick wall.

"Finished?"

"Yeah, and so are you," Frank responded.

Dutch just smiled, turned on his heel, and headed for the door.

"Hey, Dutch, if you be a good little moulie, maybe I'll let you be my lawn jockey."

Frank and his cronies rolled to that, their fat bellies shaking, doubled over with laughter. But Dutch didn't even turn around. He kept on walking. Craze lingered momentarily and caught Frank eyeing him, then Frank threw Craze a kiss.

The kiss of death.

Craze nodded slowly, then walked out behind Dutch. Frank watched as the door closed behind them. He meant every word of what he had said. He had every intention of eating away at Dutch's foundation until he had reduced him to the status Frank thought he deserved, a no-count black bum.

Frank secretly feared the repercussions of killing Dutch. So instead, he settled on making him suffer. But Frank made one fatal mistake. He underestimated Dutch.

Two weeks later, he got the picture, and he realized just who he was playing games with, and it hit him like a hard, black fist.

Frank had just woken up. He turned on the television to Channel 9 as he usually did and prepared to start his day. As he poured his morning coffee, he couldn't help overhearing the news broadcast.

"Yes, George, I'm standing here about half a block away from where police have blocked off the area. We're not yet exactly sure what has happened here. What has been confirmed is that a man, apparently strapped with explosives, walked into the police precinct during the morning shift change and detonated the bomb he was wearing."

Frank stared at the screen in disbelief. The background behind the reporter was rubble and smoke. He couldn't even recognize the building at first. He saw EMT workers pulling body after body out of the wreckage. The whole area buzzed with activity as police, firemen, and ambulance workers combed the scene for survivors. His phone rang, and it took several rings for him to realize it. He walked over to the phone and picked it up.

"Yeah . . . yeah, I see it. Who the fuck you think? . . . No . . . no, gimme a minute, nine-thirty," he said, hanging up the phone as he gazed at the screen . . .

He had underestimated Dutch.

The nigga was definitely playing by a different set of rules, which forced Frank to revise his. He knew if he didn't act quickly, Dutch would instill fear in any and all who were woven into the city's fabric. He who controlled the fabric would control the city, and Frank couldn't let Dutch destroy his plans. He went over to the phone and started dialing a number. A young woman answered.

"District attorney's office," the voice smoothly said.

"Yeah, I need to speak to Anthony Jacobs."

Frank took one last look at the screen. *Yeah kid, you definitely got balls, but I can still squeeze.*

Three months later, Dutch was arrested in his restaurant on Clinton Avenue.

The streets went crazy when news of Dutch's arrest hit the airwaves. People came out their homes and were crying in the streets, others cheered, some thanked God, and others came out of hiding.

No matter what the reaction, everybody was talking. The police precinct bombing was a tragedy. Twenty-eight police officers dead, and many others severely injured. No one walked out of the building that day, no one.

It was terrible. The mayor called a press conference in front of the bombed police precinct where so many had died.

"When the criminals representing the drug element in our society feel free to use terrorist tactics in order to fight their drug wars or to send a message, then we must come together in this tragic time and send them a message right back, that this won't be tolerated!"

The bystanders and family members of the fallen officers applauded the mayor until a young, eager reporter stepped in.

"Excuse me, Mr. Mayor. Mr. Mayor, isn't it true that Dutch played a major role in your campaign for election, sir?"

Across town on Irving Turner Boulevard, in a small bar, the press conference played out on TV as a ragged old man in a war-torn fatigue jacket sat at the bar watching the mayor stutter during the press conference. He sat sipping on some Jim Beam liquor when he heard his name, Bernard James, on the television. He looked up to see Dutch being led in handcuffs from a detective's car into 32 Green Street.

"He fightin' the war, too. But dat dere boy, see, he gonna win. We gonna win this war yet!" he exclaimed in a drunken slur.

"Huh?" The bartender looked at him.

"I said, we gonna win this war yet," he repeated, downing the rest of his drink in one gulp.

The bartender knew the old soldier well. He had been coming in for as long as he could remember. He knew the old man was shell-shocked from the war. He often talked to himself, cried to himself, even laughed to himself, but he never got excited the way he was now.

"Ain't no war, old man. The Vietnam War ended damn near thirty years ago," the bartender said as he walked down the bar, shaking his head.

"Man, it's a war going on out here. Listen to Marvin Gaye. He knew, too," the old man said, lighting another cigarette.

"How the hell you gonna tell me. I know it's a war going on out there and we gonna win it yet." Then he smiled, and anyone who knew would have said he smiled just like Dutch.

Even Cherry Martinez spread the news on the radio.

"Yo! Y'all ain't gonna believe this, but guess who just got bagged? Dutch! Yes, y'all heard it here first, they done got Dutch. But you know how it goes. So Dutch, darling, if you're listenin' just know the streets is wit' you, baby. Matter of fact, I'ma play a joint a little birdie told me used to be your theme song, Kool G Rap's 'Road to the Riches.' Stay up, Poppi, from your girl, Cherry 'Da Bomb' Martinez, droppin' it for you like that on your favorite radio station."

Kool G Rap must've played for an hour on various stations in New York. It was crazy. You would've thought the man had died. Dutch probably couldn't hear Cherry or any of the other radio stations, but Craze certainly did.

He turned up the volume as he headed toward Chancellor Avenue in his Porsche, a five-car convoy behind him. He had business to handle.

Young street wolves were smelling blood . . .

Dutch's.

And they were prepared to feast. While Dutch was in jail for two weeks, Craze handled the business and held it down. Everyone knew what was at stake, but no one was really in position to make anything happen.

No one except Rock and Roll.

Rock and Roll were two aspiring rap artists who had just gotten a record deal with a major label. Basically, they were two ex-stickup artists who got in the game around the same time the Zoo Crew was coming up. They had a strong team with enough heart and enough money to become a formidable opponent to try to fill the void Dutch was about to leave.

But Dutch wasn't gone yet, and Craze was that crazy nigga to dig all up in your ass. He had found out from one of the Charlies who was tricking the nigga Roll that they were planning to kill him and some of the members of the Zoo Crew once Dutch was safely behind bars. Once Craze got wind of that information, he went into action immediately.

He rounded up one of Dutch's favorites from Prince Street, a young kid by the name of Young World. World was up and coming, and Dutch was real big on that nigga. World's murder game and his rep in the street was remarkable.

Within an hour of Craze's call, he and his own street team pulled up to Roll's candy store on Chancellor Avenue. When Craze walked in, Roll had his back to the door and was talking on the pay phone. By the time he noticed Craze's presence, Craze had his gun drawn. Young World and his twelve-man army guarded the streets and the door. When Roll finally turned around, he found a nine-millimeter pointed at his face.

"See how easy it is, muhfucka! How you gonna kill somebody if you already dead, huh?"

"Craze, wha—" His sentence was cut short by a hard backhand. Craze followed with a blow from the pistol handle to his head. Roll fell up against the counter.

"Fuck you think, this shit's a game? You think you gonna kill me, nigga? What you waitin' for, pussy?" Craze shouted.

"Naw, Craze, please don't kill me. It ain't like that, I swear." He was once again cut off by a blow from Craze. This time, Craze pressed his foot into Roll's midsection so hard it made Roll crumple into a fetal position on the floor and gasp for air.

"Don't lie to me, muhfucka! I got ears everywhere, nigga!"

While Craze continued stomping Roll, World and his team had been carrying all the candy and soda to the door, throwing it in the street for the little kids. They came from everywhere, laughing and grabbing up the candy, then running off, knowing they were wrong. Craze flipped open the cash register and counted.

"Nigga, this all you got? Fuckin' chump-change-ass nigga, gonna kill me!"

Craze laughed as he dragged the badly beaten Roll out the door.

"Yo, give me the keys to that nigga shit," said World with a devilish grin on his face, ready to see if he could still 360.

Craze dug the keys out of Roll's pocket and threw them to World. He then pushed Roll onto the hood of the car and started stripping him of his jewelry.

"Fuckin' clown-ass nigga! Fuck is you stupid? You better stick to that rap shit, muhfucker!"

"Craze, man, it ain't like that," Roll slurred through swollen lips.

"You stupid, nigga, why you lyin'? Your own man, Rock, told me what was up," Craze lied.

Roll looked at him silently.

"Oh, you think I'm lyin'? The nigga sold you out. He

came and told me it was all your idea, tryin' to get down with us."

·"I—I don't know what you talkin' 'bout," Roll said innocently, but Craze knew he was lying.

"That's on you, dog. I'm just pullin' your coat to your man, 'cause yous'a clown-ass nigga and so is your man. But, yo, if I'm lyin' then who else knew?"

Roll looked up at Craze and he could tell that his last statement had struck a nerve. Craze looked at Young World's crazy ass speeding up and down the block on Roll's Ninja bike. World was doughnuting and leaving tire tracks in the middle of the street and Craze smiled to himself. *Dutch taught that nigga well.*

"The weakest part of a motherfucker is his mind. Control that and ain't no gun more powerful than that," he remembered Dutch once saying. As he looked in Roll's face, he could tell Dutch had been right. A few weeks later, Rock and Roll had so much beef the duo split and lost their recording contract.

Divide and conquer.

But the streets weren't the only ones making plans in Dutch's absence. Frank Sorbonno and the Nigerians had a few tricks left up their sleeves.

Mr. Odouwo had contacted Frank and asked him to meet him at his hotel suite at the W in Times Square. Frank arrived accompanied by one of his bodyguards. Mr. Odouwo appeared to be alone, but Frank knew he wasn't. Nigerians had a peculiar way of dealing that Frank had never quite gotten used to.

He walked over to the table laid out with fruit and

Danish, shook Mr. Odouwo's hand, and sat down. Mr. Odouwo finished pouring them each a glass of wine, then he sat as well.

"I thank you, Mr. Sorbonno, for meeting with me, despite our past differences. I hope the fruits of this council will assuage any ill feelings between us," he said, raising his glass for a toast before sipping.

"For years, we have had Mr. James's name written on our hearts . . . the part reserved for vengeance. Ojiugo Kazami was one of our dearest countrymen. He served us well and to know he died in such a way to a man such as Mr. James, well . . . is a blow to our pride, to say the very least. And we would have implemented swift justice had it not been for your people's protection. Yet we knew it would only be a matter of time before someone more sympathetic to our concerns would take over, for a house divided cannot stand," said Mr. Odouwo, knowing the hand Frank played in Tony's death, but not yet revealing it.

"But it seems God has smiled on us, as I understand Mr. Cerone is no longer with us."

"Yeah, the bastard finally caught it."

"So, what do you intend to do?" Mr. Odouwo asked.

"I wanna kill the little black son of a bitch!" Frank blurted out before realizing who he was talking to. "No offense."

"None taken." The Nigerian smiled, then continued. "But, let me be honest, heroin is our biggest export—that is, after oil. We use the proceeds to fund our freedom fighters back in my country. So, the trade here in New Jersey is important to us. Therefore, I ask that you leave the streets and Mr. James to us. While your vendetta is personal, ours is, shall I say, spiritual. In return, I invite you to Nigeria.

It is a beautiful country, the most beautiful in the world. I invite you to partake of its splendor. There are many opportunities for a man such as yourself in my country." Mr. Odouwo smiled, knowing Frank had no options.

Mr. Odouwo had Frank's deck of cards in his hands, and if Frank didn't agree, he would find out just how dangerous the Odouwo crime family was. Besides, Mr. Odouwo was well aware that it was Frankie Bonno who had the two hits put out on his friend and business partner, Ojiugo. Frank was lucky he was still breathing.

Frank just looked at him, and his thoughts went to Dutch. To him, an unlikely alliance was about to be struck based on the hatred of one man. It was then Frank realized that both hemispheres of the globe had been affected by the cancer called Dutch.

Frank stuck out his hand and the bargain was sealed. Frank would send Dutch to prison, while the Nigerians would send him to his grave.

CHAPTER THIRTEEN

◆

CLOSING STATEMENTS

The community and media were staked outside the courtroom in anticipation of the verdict.

Guilty.

The police controlled the streets with barriers as a mob formed outside the courthouse. Inside the courthouse, Frank Sorbonno sat in the courtroom waiting patiently. His mind told him not to come, but his pride chided him to attend. He had to be there, to see firsthand when the jurors took away Dutch's life and his freedom. He wanted to see the look in Dutch's eyes. He had to; there was no way in the world he was going to miss it.

Jacobs entered the courtroom like the king of France. He knew he had the case sewn up; he could smell the aroma of victory. He had promised several reporters one-on-one interviews after the trial, and later, he had already arranged for a professional call girl to call on him at a suite he'd rented under an assumed name in the Trump Plaza overlooking Central Park.

He thought of Old Man Ligotta. *I know you're smilin', old*

man. He then began walking up the aisle, viewing all those present, and caught the eye of Frank Sorbonno and smirked. Frank returned the gesture with a wink of his eye. *Lot of elderly here today,* thought Jacobs. They all seemed so motionless.

Then it hit him, as he looked one in the face he saw her hair was gray and her figure matronly, but she had none of the telltale signs of aging. He shrugged her off, figuring she was the mother or grandmother of one of Dutch's many victims.

Jacobs made his way over to the prosecutor's table and looked over at Dutch and his law team. As Glass whispered to Dutch, Jacobs and Dutch made eye contact for the first and last time that day.

I got you, you black bastard, Jacobs's sneer seemed to say.

Dutch responded silently with his eyes. *Oh, really.*

Glass turned around to see Dutch was smiling at Jacobs. Glass nodded to Jacobs, who nodded back at him, then he turned to Dutch.

In his heart of hearts, Glass knew they had lost the trial. They lost the trial with Reverend Taylor. Perhaps if Dutch had let him cross-examine the reverend the outcome would have been different. But it started there and went quickly downhill for Glass, who had planned on this moment being a joyous occasion and major career boost.

But he knew it wasn't going to happen.

The judge walked in.

"All rise," said the bailiff as the judge made his way to his bench.

"You may be seated," said the judge after he sat. "Bring in the jury," he commanded.

Within moments, the jury was reseated. The judge turned to Glass.

"Are you prepared to proceed with your closing statements, Counselor?"

"Yes, Your Honor, I am," Glass replied with confidence.

He stood up and looked at the jury. No one could blame him for the outcome of the trial. His performance had been impeccable. So he decided to remove himself from Dutch's destiny and went on to deliver the most eloquent closing statement of his career.

"Ladies and gentlemen of the jury. You have just sat through three weeks of the biggest and baddest gangster movie ever performed. It was better than *The Godfather* and better than *Casino.* It reminded me of *Scarface* . . . and just as fictitious. It was written, directed, and produced by your own district attorney, Anthony Jacobs. He deserves an Oscar," said Glass as he watched the jury and detected several amused expressions.

Jacobs knew he had overdone it just a little with his theatrics from time to time, but the end would justify the means. He believed in killing a mosquito with an axe.

"But this isn't Hollywood, ladies and gentlemen. There is a man's life at stake. These past few weeks, not a single fact has been presented by Attorney Jacobs, not one. He has merely presented circumstantial evidence held together by the weak glue of assumptions. Assumptions of crooked cops, gangsters turned ministers, five-and-dime hustlers . . . not one law-abiding citizen in the bunch. He brings waywardness in the guise of truth and twists every word that comes out of his mouth to lure you away from what's real, what's true. The witnesses he's produced certainly aren't credible enough to hang a man's life on."

He walked over to his table, looked at Dutch, sipped from a glass of water, then turned back to the jurors.

"The district attorney has not proven Mr. James committed any crimes. What crimes did he commit? I still don't know. And it is supposed to be your job to find out based on the evidence supplied by the state. I don't think so. I don't think this jury should confuse the manuscript Attorney Jacobs has presented with the real facts of this case." Glass paused, then walked back over to the jurors' box.

"If you do that, then you can only see my client's innocent of these charges!" he said sternly, staring down the throats of each and every one of the jurors as if they had better not find his client guilty.

"Thank you," he added, readjusting his tie as he slowly walked back to the defense table. He knew it wasn't looking good for the home team, but for himself, it was of the utmost importance. Maybe Dutch's career was about to be over, but his was not; it was just beginning.

The blare of the car horn brought Nina out of her reverie. She glanced into her rearview mirror as she pulled off. She hadn't seen Dutch since the day she showed him her brother's mural some time ago. She tried calling him, but the number she had for him was disconnected.

She wanted to see him, in spite of everything that had been written in the paper every day since Dutch's case went to trial. None of it mattered. She missed Dutch, and more important, she wanted to be with him. She tried not to think of him, but the media attention and press coverage were everywhere and everyone gossiped daily about the police precinct bombing and the trial.

On the news at six and eleven, Dutch was constantly referred to as a gangster or as a "notorious drug lord," or as the "chief orchestrator" of the Month of Murder. He was everywhere, and she knew he needed her. He had sent letters to her by courier at her job asking her to meet him in certain places for lunch, but she never went. She never met him, and after a while, his letters stopped. That's when she tried to call him.

If only I had met him at Chin Chin. I should have met him. What was I thinking? Questions like that repeated in Nina's mind. She thought about all the opportunities she had had to be with him. How he had sweated her to death when they first met, and how sincere and honest he had always been with her about his feelings.

As she made her way to the courthouse, she pleaded with God for the chance to tell Dutch how she really felt about him.

Jacobs was thoroughly impressed with Glass's closing statement. *Won't change nothing though.* Jacobs couldn't help thinking that to himself. He would have been worried had the situation been different. But there was nothing Glass could have said to change the course of the trial or of his career. Jacobs was going places, and he knew it. He stood up slowly, cleared his throat, and began his closing statement.

"Ladies and gentlemen of the jury. I thank you for your time and patience throughout these past few weeks. As I said in the beginning, there are a lot of other things we could have been doing, but we had our duty to one another and ourselves," he said, quickly scanning the two rows of jurors.

"Yes, the last few weeks have been submerged in the murky waters of Bernard James's life, his disregard for life, law and order, and the property of others. From his youth and stealing cars to the present, his existence has been filled with bloodshed, murder, innocent victims, and shattered lives." He stopped for a moment to catch his breath as he looked at the twelve faces that would make him famous.

"You must do for Simone Smith, her mother, and her father, what they are not here to do today. Remember Detective O'Neal from the Twenty-ninth Precinct, the survivors, and their family members," Jacobs said, glancing at Frankie Bonno, who smiled inwardly.

"Your duty is to them now. Your duty is to honor the memory of each and every life Bernard James has taken," Jacobs said, leaning on the rail of the jury box.

"Because if you don't . . . then the lives he'll take in the future will be blood on your hands. Let's hope and pray his next victim isn't one of you, one of your children, your mother, your father, your sister, your brother, or your wife or husband," Jacobs said, pointing at the jurors.

"If we do not have justice and find the defendant, Bernard James, guilty today, then each and every one of you will leave this courtroom as guilty as that man right there!" he ended, pointing at Dutch, his closing statement just as theatrical as his entire trial.

Jacobs went back to the prosecutor's table and sat down. He could have continued, but why? He had the case in the bag. Hands down, he knew he had won.

The jurors sat still, waiting and wondering if he was finished.

"Thank you, Attorney Jacobs," the judge concluded, making sure it was clear he was finished with his closing statement.

"Your Honor." Jacobs stood, nodded at the judge, then sat back down.

"Ah, Your Honor, my client would like to . . . ahhh, address the court," Glass requested as he glanced down at Dutch.

The judge looked down at Dutch in curiosity, inwardly smiling. He, too, had grown to despise Dutch after listening to the past few weeks of testimony. He knew that Dutch would now beg for mercy, which he would, of course, deny. He wanted the press and everyone in the courtroom to witness it.

"Is this true, Mr. James?"

"Yes, Your Honor."

The judge glanced at Glass, who didn't have a clue. Then he looked at Jacobs, who subtly nodded, with an amused expression on his face.

"This is a highly unusual request at this stage in the trial, but I will allow it. You may proceed, Mr. James."

Dutch swiveled in the wooden chair before slowly standing up and facing the jury.

"I'm not gonna take up much of your time. Especially since I know what you're thinking. I can see it in your eyes. You're dyin' to say it, too. Guilty," Dutch said, looking at each and every last one of the jurors prepared to send him to prison for the rest of his life or worse, sentence him to the death penalty.

"See? It ain't hard to tell. So, since we both know how you feel, I guess I'm suppose to throw myself on your mercy, have remorse and sorrow, and say I'm sorry and beg you not to find me guilty?"

Dutch chuckled lightly and shook his head slowly, answering his own question.

"Naw . . . naw, I'll let God judge me. But to you, I only got one thing to say: Fuck all y'all."

The courtroom was buzzing in astonishment. The judge looked at Dutch with contempt, but Dutch just laughed. He laughed louder and harder at the judge. The courtroom became silent at his maddening laughter, and the judge continued to bang his gavel, requesting that Glass silence his client or he would be held in contempt of court.

"Dutch, please, the judge," Glass said as Dutch stopped laughing. Glass was thankful. But just as he became silent, Dutch reached into his pocket and pulled out a cigar and a lighter. He lit the tip of the cigar . . .

CLICK! CLICK! CLICK! The sounds of automatic weapons were ominous. No one moved. Even the judge stopped banging his gavel as he heard the sounds.

Frankie Bonno's gut told him he should have stayed home, but his pride, his pride, had him right where Dutch wanted him.

Anthony Jacobs, who felt like a man on the verge of success and status . . . only ran out of time.

Everyone in the courtroom lived different lives. Those last few moments, those last few thoughts, sealed time forever as the sound of gunfire shattered the silence like glass.

CHAPTER FOURTEEN

◆

THE REACTION

Yes, Bob, I'm standing outside the Essex County Court-house in Newark, New Jersey, and as you can see from the number of police cars and ambulances, there has been an unbelievable tragedy here today.

"The trial of Bernard James ended in gunfire only moments ago; details are sketchy. But this is what we do know. The gunfire started from somewhere inside the courtroom among the spectators. We are not sure how many, but we do know several spectators opened fire inside the courtroom.

"Among those confirmed dead are Frank Sorbonno, alleged crime boss of the Cerone crime family. Also, confirmed dead: Judge Whitaker, the judge who presided over the case. Eight members of the jury—I'm sorry, Bob, make that nine out of the twelve jurors are dead. Their names, however, are being withheld until contact has been made with family members. The other three members of the jury have been rushed to St. Agnes Hospital with gunshot wounds, and we are waiting for an update on their conditions. As soon as we have more details, we will report them to you."

• • •

One-eyed Roc had just gotten out of Jumah, the Islamic prayer service held in the prison every Friday at 1:00 P.M. He walked down the hall, curious as to what was going on. Everyone was hyped up and loud; laughter rang as he returned to his cell and everyone was happy, open, and excited, like there was a party going on.

"Yo, Roc, you ain't heard?" asked some guy named Detroit as he ran up to Roc.

"Heard what? I been in Jumah for the past hour and a half."

"Your man, Dutch! Yo, your man went all out! Nigga, shot up the courtroom, killed the judge, the jury, some mob muhfucker, everybody. Then he got away!"

"Naw, naw, it ain't go down like that," said some other nigga who overheard Detroit and butted in. "The nigga ain't get away," the man said, clearing up the misconception.

"Man, I heard the shit with my own two ears, fuck you talkin' bout?" Detroit replied in an annoyed tone. He didn't know where the guy came from or where he was getting his information.

"You ain't hear that! I'm tryin' to tell you what the fuck I know."

Roc could see that the two men were about to begin arguing, so he walked away, shaking his head.

Shot up the courtroom? And a mobster? Who they talkin' 'bout, Frankie Bonno? Roc thought as he made his way into his cell. He quickly turned on the radio and searched the dial, until he heard . . .

"We now know the identity of the shooters. There were approximately twelve in all, dressed as old ladies. They are believed to be members of an alleged group of women assassins. They call themselves Angel's Charlies, their name courtesy of Angel Alvirez, a Hispanic woman who two years ago was convicted of killing a federal agent in a shootout in the St. Agnes Hospital parking lot and given multiple life sentences. At least seven of these women are confirmed dead. In total, eighteen people are dead. We are still waiting to learn what is known of Bernard James, aka Dutch . . ."

Nina drove with her every thought on Dutch. Yes, she had finally made up her mind. She thought of the commitment she was making, the visits, the absentee holidays, the appeal denials, the disappointments, the dream, all of it. She was prepared . . . until she heard the reporter on the radio.

"Yes, this is Miriam Roughneen reporting for Channel 11 news from the Essex County Courthouse where today's trial ended in a deadly bloodbath."

In a daze, she heard the reporter but couldn't believe what was said. Tears welled in her eyes. It hit her. It was over. There would be no remorse for Dutch, no other side of the game for him. He wouldn't be going to prison, and she wouldn't have to worry about the long trips to be by his side.

She listened as the reporter ran off names of the dead, and she prayed his was not included. A horn honked behind her, and she pulled her car over to the side of the road. She couldn't drive, her emotions wouldn't let her, and as she realized the reality of the situation tears began to stream down her face.

The reporter finished the list of names. Nina prayed that she wouldn't say Dutch's, and she didn't. Relief filled her, and she thanked God, knowing that they were destined to be together. She put the car in drive and headed to the courthouse.

Delores Murphy stood looking out the window of her penthouse apartment. The news played on the television behind her. She, too, heard the news and she felt heavy with grief. Grief because she felt the loss of her only son beginning to consume her. It was too much and merely a matter of time.

There were too many murders and too many lives taken by the hand of one man. Dutch had caused tremendous pain and anguish, and Delores wished her son some peace. Yes, she wished peace for those who had suffered by his hand, too.

The reporter's voice could be heard coming from the television speakers.

"Bob, I have a breaking update surrounding the trial of the century."

Delores turned to watch the television, unable to think of anything else.

"We have with us Detective Edward Smalls. Detective Smalls, can you tell us what is happening?" the reporter asked.

"This was certainly a tragedy no one expected. Somehow, Mr. James had smuggled automatic weapons through the elaborate detection system of the courthouse. We are trying to get all the facts at this time."

"Our sources confirm the deaths of Frank Sorbonno, Judge Whitak—"

Detective Smalls cut the reporter off. "District Attorney Anthony Jacobs is also among the dead . . . excuse me," he said, speaking quickly to someone standing behind him.

Detective Smalls stepped to the side while a uniformed officer whispered in his ear. He looked confused, then nodded and returned to the reporter.

"We now have information on Bernard James."

"I told you he wasn't dead!" Jazz shouted.

"They ain't say he wasn't!" Moet responded just as loudly.

"Yo, World! World, tell this stupid muhfucka that niggas like Dutch don't die!" Jazz said, turning to Young World.

Young World looked around at his young team of wolves. They were all just like him. He had schooled them all and he had learned from the best . . .

Dutch.

World was only nineteen, but he was black, hungry, and hopeless, which in the ghetto meant dangerous. He already knew what he wanted. Lil' Kim sang it to him all the time.

Money . . . Power . . . Respect.

World had started on Dutch's street team on Hawthorne, but when Roc fell, Dutch gave World Roc's spot on Prince also. Dutch liked World. He spent many a night with him explaining and priming the young hustler. Young World thought back to their last conversation.

"The streets is gonna be wide open like pussy after this. Niggas you thought you could count on either gonna flip and try and go for dolo or nut-up under pressure. And everybody gonna claim they speakin' for me or on my behalf. Shit is gonna be crazy," Dutch told him.

"Now ain't nothing I can do for you, you can't do for yourself, but I'ma give you somethin' for you to remember me by," he added, handing Young World a large duffel bag.

"The rest is up to you, lil' man," Dutch said, ending the conversation.

Young World stood still as the television continued reporting on the trial of the century, as it was now being referred to. He had the duffel bag that Dutch had given him in his hands. Everyone was curious to know what was in the bag, even World himself. He still hadn't looked in it. With Dutch, you never knew. So just in case that crazy nigga wanted his bag back, World considered himself holding it for a minute.

"Yo, World, you think he dead or what?" Jazz repeated.

Young World gazed at Jazz, his right-hand man. He knew if anybody flipped, it wouldn't be Jazz or anybody in the room . . . they were a family to one another.

Young World was about to finally answer, but before he could, the reporter came back on TV.

"Detective Smalls, before you were called away, you said that you had information on Bernard James?"

"Yes, we do. Bernard James is dead. We just found his body."

"Detective Smalls of the Newark Police Department has just informed me that Bernard James is in fact dead. A tragic day here in Essex County. We'll keep you posted . . ."

Young World's street team all lowered their heads. They couldn't believe their ears, but they had all heard it. Young World laid the duffel bag on the table and the sound of its zipper caught everyone's attention. Young World reached in the bag and pulled out a .32 automatic. It was the gun that

Dutch had used in his first murder. Then he began pulling out stack after stack of money, totaling five hundred thousand dollars. Then he reached in the bag and pulled out Dutch's crown . . .

Kazami's infamous dragon chain.

World slowly put the chain around his neck as if it had belonged to him all along. Everybody stared at him in awe. They knew the two men who had worn that chain and what it meant.

Young World glanced down at the chain. He thought of Dutch, and all the things the man had taught him over the years. He felt honored to be the one left holding the dragon chain, and he meant to hold the position Dutch had left behind.

He placed the plate-sized charm under the light and watched the diamonds and rubies dance.

"Ain't no turnin' back now. We 'bout to get this shit on and poppin'. Anybody feel different, need to bounce now," said World, ready to play his position.

No one moved.

Qwan was sitting at his desk in his large church office watching CNN when he heard the news. He thought back to the day he saw Dutch in court, when he was testifying against him. No matter what, Dutch had always had his back, and what he did in the courtroom proved it. Qwan felt in his heart he had done the right thing, but he also knew in his heart that he had betrayed a friend. A good friend.

He hit the off button on the remote and watched as the television screen faded to darkness. He did not want to hear any more about the trial or about Dutch. It was all a part of the past now, or at least for him it was. He had made his peace with his past. It had haunted him for so long, but now he felt he could let go. And his demons were exactly where he wanted them, in the past.

He bowed his head and said a short prayer for Dutch's soul.

Delores Murphy stood frozen and still. Her heart became saddened as she heard the detective say her son's dead body had been recovered. For Dutch, she would be strong. There would be no tears for Delores, only another ache to add to her long list of life's disappointments.

You kept your promise though and died free. You didn't let them lock you up. You put up a fight. I love you, son.

She felt her eyes begin to draw tears. She wiped them, quickly, then walked into her kitchen to make a cup of tea.

Delores was from that era when black was power and freedom was all you had. But a black man never had any real freedom and still doesn't. Back in Delores's day, freedom was something to fight for if you wanted it. Delores and her generation were that generation of people who fought. The Malcolm Xs, the Huey Newtons, the Black Panthers, and so forth fought in their day; they just didn't win.

They fought a war that never got printed in the history books or taught in the public school system. However, Delores kept notes. And today her son would not go to a white man's prison and be a slave. She was honored by his exit.

She smiled, then sipped her tea.

O'Neal sat in his living room watching Channel 9 report the news from the courthouse. It was finally over. He looked down at his missing legs in his wheelchair. He had felt the pain of his loss every day since the police precinct bombing. It had literally shattered his world. Never being able to walk again was something he still hadn't come to terms with. He stared at the television as the reporter spoke of the dead body of Bernard James, which had just been found.

He smiled, held up the beer he was drinking in a mock toast, and said his own little prayer for Dutch.

"Burn in hell, nigger." He laughed.

Mrs. Piazza switched the television to another channel, searching for more news on the trial of the century and Dutch. Her phone rang, but she did not answer.

Thank you, Dutch. She spoke to herself as tears streamed down her face for Dutch.

She hadn't returned to the courthouse after seeing Dutch, but she thought of him every day. Dutch, to her, was like the son she never had.

When Roberto had the heart attack, Dutch rushed to the County Memorial Hospital emergency ward. He stayed with Roberto, by Mrs. Piazza's side.

"Dutch, go on now, go home, get some rest. I'll be fine," whispered Mrs. Piazza, as she placed a warm hand on his back.

"How can I leave him like this? He's the only man that's been in my life since I was young, and now I'm a grown man. He's the only man I've ever known to look out for me like a father and I know that if it were me, he'd stay," said Dutch, his eyes filled with tears for Roberto. Mrs. Piazza put her arms around Dutch and hugged him tightly, holding her close to him.

"Stay."

When he died, Dutch stayed right by her side as he knew Roberto would have wanted. She had her sisters and his family, of course. But there was a special bond she and Dutch shared. She remembered their last meeting prior to the trial.

A few weeks after Fat Tony's death, Mrs. Piazza called Dutch and told him to meet her at the pizza shop. When he got there, the lights were off, but the door was left open.

He walked into the parlor and flipped the light switch on the wall, but the lights did not come on.

"Dutch, come in. I'm in the back."

"Mrs. Piazza," Dutch called out as he nervously moved in the dark to the sound of her voice.

She lit a lighter and he saw her face behind the flame.

"Mrs. Piazza, you okay?" Dutch asked, bending his head and looking at her, somewhat confused.

"You must leave, Dutch. Frankie Bonno has set you up to fall. He's paid the prosecutor's office to investigate you. They're going to indict you and put you in prison, where you will be murdered. The other families, well, what can I say, they agreed."

"Did they agree to this before or after Fat Tony's death?"

"Dutch, you know the answer to that. Fat Tony's death changed a lot of things for everyone, not just you," she said, thinking of the loss Fat Tony represented to all.

She looked at him confused, wondering if he understood. If Fat Tony was dead, and Frankie Bonno was still walking, it wasn't too hard to figure out what the families had agreed to.

"Go, please. You must leave, now. Get yourself out of the country while you can," she ordered him.

"I can't leave, but I thank you. You've always been there for me. You're like a mother to me, you know that?" he asked, looking into her watery eyes.

"You're like a son to me, too. You know that, Dutch, like a son," she said putting her arms around him and cradling him in her arms, desperate for his future.

She was risking her life meeting him. But she knew it was the right thing to do, just as Dutch had saved her life so many years ago. She had every intention of returning the favor.

"I love you, Dutch. You take care of yourself, *capisce?*"

"Si, *capisco.*"

Mrs. Piazza took his face in her hands and kissed Dutch's right cheek, then his left, before letting his face go. He took her hands into his and removed the lighter she was holding.

"I need this, Miriam," he said. He had never before called her by her first name.

"Wha'? You don't smoke. You startin' fires, now?" she asked jokingly as she handed it to him.

"I'm 'bout to," he said, smiling his infamous smile, letting her know he had it all under control.

She grabbed a tissue and wiped the tears from her eyes and face. *Oh, Dutch, if only you had listened to me.* She grabbed the remote to the television and pressed the off button.

By the time Nina reached the courthouse, the police had blocked off the area. Luckily, she found parking, and it was then that she heard the reporter speaking with Detective Smalls.

"We just found his body." Those were the words still ringing through her body. She dropped her small purse on the passenger seat as her body went limp. She had never gotten the chance to tell him how she felt. How she wished to be with him. Now, he was gone.

Nina bent her head as tears began to stream down her face. She felt the same pain and shed the same tears as she had for her brother, so long ago.

Angel sat on her bunk listening to NPR News. She heard the words, but it didn't register. *Dutch, dead? He can't be,* and her mind would not allow her to associate the two. *Dutch can't die.* She wouldn't let him. She felt her chest tighten as she balled up her fist, and she tried to hold back tears. She had not cried in over twenty years. She wanted to hit something, hard, to let out the pain. She hit her pillow, then began swinging the pillow harder and harder onto the metal railing of the bunkbed until the pillow burst open and its stuffing showered the cell like rain. *I love you, Dutch,* she silently thought.

In his hotel suite, Mr. Odouwu received a phone call, informing him about the news of Dutch. He hung up the phone and smiled lightly as he poured himself a Scotch. Taking a sip, he went back to the phone, dialed a number, and waited for an answer.

"Book me a flight to France, right away," he ordered, then hung up the phone.

• • •

"See, I knew it. I knew that soldier was a fighter. God damn, we fighting a war and we done started winnin' now!" yelled the war-torn soldier, still sitting at the bar.

"I told you, old man, the war is over, calm down," said the bartender from the other end of the bar.

"Man, you must not be able to see what I do."

"See what?"

"See," said the old man. Then he smiled . . . just like Dutch.

The news of Dutch's death went through the city like an electrical current. Everyone felt the shocking effect of his demise and the void left behind. There were eight million stories told at his wake. The police kept vigil on the streets in hope of preventing the rise of the next young hustler trying to walk in his footsteps. But none would ever fill his shoes.

Dutch was a legend.

He had promised himself never to return to jail. He said he'd hold court in the streets. But the truth was, he had held the streets in court.

EPILOGUE

♦

DON DIVA INTERVIEW . . . ONE YEAR LATER

I went to see Rahman Muhammad at the federal penitentiary in Lewisburg, Pennsylvania. He had contacted me and informed me he would like to do the interview that I had proposed to him a week before. Rahman Muhammad, aka "One-eyed Roc," was one of the original members of Dutch's New Jersey clique. He is now Muslim, and is serving several life sentences.

He walked into the visitation booth and picked up the phone. Our visit was held in a booth separated by six-inch-thick Plexiglas. Communication was facilitated by phones on both sides of the glass.

Don Diva: What up, bruh?

Rahman: I'm chillin' . . . Under the circumstances.

DD: Underdug and overstood. How did you lose your eye?

R: It happened when I was about eight, me and my cousin were playing with firecrackers on the roof of my building. It happened then.

DD: Oh, i'ight. Yo, bruh, I've been trying to get wit' cha for a minute—why now?

R: Because . . . I got somethin' to say. I feel like I owe it to a lot of people, who knew who I was—to know who I am now, 'cause, you know, my parents, they tried to raise me in Islam. My wife always tried to get me on my deen, but them streets had me, now the beast got me. My kids [Rahman has three] don't have a father and my wife has no husband and I think the world should know why. Maybe they won't make the same mistakes.

DD: Tell me how you met Dutch.

R: I met Dutch maybe fifteen years ago, when we were both stealin' cars. I was probably no more than fourteen at the time. See, we were stealin' cars for fun, you know, doin' tricks and outrunnin' 5-0, but Dutch, he had a connect. Now back then, it was damn near impossible for little cats like us to have a chop-shop connect. So Dutch went around the whole city, collecting the best little tackhead car thieves he knew about, and my name rang bells back then for being one of the nicest.

DD: Didn't Dutch go to jail for stealing cars?

R: Yeah, but for the city, it was the worst mistake they could've made. See, Dutch was always smart. I don't know if he ever took an IQ test, but there's no doubt in my mind he was a genius. He knew cats' hearts, [he] knew how to manipulate and strategize. He was a cold-blooded individual, but he was no fool. There was definitely a method to his madness.

DD: Madness like the "Month of Murder"?

R: The Month of Murder was like . . . like a military coup. Kazami [a murdered Newark drug lord] was king, and when he fell, all the king's horses and all his men had to go with him. Anybody loyal to that regime was erased and replaced. See, 'cause you had a lot of cats who wanted the crown, too. Kids was plottin' left and right. Like Money-Murph, in Jersey City. Dutch knew Jersey City was gonna be hardheaded 'cause the beef between J.C. and Newark is legendary. Wasn't no Newark nigga gonna run J.C. But Dutch came and got me on a Ninja and we rode to Jersey City, right into Kurrywoods, one of the roughest projects there. He rode right up on Murph and his people. Now keep in mind, we ain't got *no* gun, no nothin', just heart. Yo, guns was clickin' everywhere 'cause these cats was ready to dead us, but Dutch took off his shirt, walked right up to Murph, and told him to shoot him a fair one. Dutch had on Kazami's dragon chain and everybody knew it. Murph just looked at the chain, so Dutch took it off. He threw it at Murph's feet and told him, "If you a 'live' nigga, lock ass and take what's yours." Yo . . . Murph shoulda just shot him then, 'cause Dutch beat son ass in front of all his people—clowned him. Just like that, Murph wasn't the man he was before, and Dutch moved into J.C. wit' ease. Real respect real.

DD: Now that's gangster.

R: Naw . . . That's Dutch. Like I said, cats respected Dutch, and in the game, that's bottom line. Machiavelli once said, *"A ruler should be feared instead of loved."* But in the game, a scared nigga'll kill you quick. Either wit' another team or wit' the police. So even though everybody didn't love Dutch, neither did everybody fear him . . . but everybody did respect him. I think that's the balance—between love and fear.

DD: Speaking of "everybody," rumor has it that more than a few record labels owe Dutch more than a thank-you card. Care to elaborate?

R: Naaw . . . But let's just say, if it wasn't for Dutch, a lot of cats, not only in entertainment, but clothing and sports, wouldn't be where they are today. Not only because of the paper Dutch put out, but [because of] the protection. Everybody thinks the Jews run the industry. They don't. They *own* it, but the mob controls it. But being under Dutch's wing, they avoided a lot of the bull crap.

DD: You mentioned the mob. I've heard it said that Dutch was the first black cat *in* the Mafia.

R: [Laughs] Naw, naw, Dutch wasn't in no Mafia.

DD: Was he connected?

R: [Rahman pauses before he answers.] Dutch was connected to a lot of people.

DD: Are you still in contact with Angel? [Angel Alvirez is the only other surviving member of the family, besides Roc. Craze hasn't been seen since the shootout at the trial.]

R: Me and Angel is always gonna be fam, but we both dealin' wit' our own issues. But I keep her in my prayers. I sent her a Quran, too.

DD: Now that you're Muslim, how do you see your former life? Is there any good that came from it?

R: In Islam, this world is called *"dunya,"* meaning "low place." I was totally *dunya*, we were totally *dunya* . . . I can't say that any good came out of that life except I learned about the mercy of Allah. When I was arrested, I had been shot by the feds. But they waited over an hour to call an ambulance, hoping I'd die. But I didn't, I'm here. Allah gave me another chance.

DD: What's the status of your appeal?

R: To be honest, I'm really not concerned with that. I'm not gonna lie and say I don't want to go home, but I really don't feel I'm ready. It's easy to be on your deen in prison, but out in that world, in the *dunya* . . . it's a whole 'nother story, especially for me. You gotta realize, since I was real young I've been spoiled by the life I led. I did what I wanted, when I wanted, and how I wanted. During the Month of Murder, me and Zoom walked up in Livingston Mall, rang they fire alarm, and in the confusion ran up in the arcade and murdered two cats from Edison, loyal to Kazami. I'm not proud of what I've done. I was sick, and I know I'm not completely cured. I need to fight my own jihad and let the Quran be my medicine.

DD: What do you want people out there to know, before we end this interview?

R: I want them to realize that, no matter how many times you get away wit' what you're doin', it *will* catch up with you. Because when it's all said and done, it's not about man's law, it's about God's law, the law of retribution. Just look at everybody who lived this life. Where they at now? Why do you think you can be any different, be the one who gets away? It's like the lottery—one out of a million hit, and that keeps the other 999,999 going broke. But you ain't playin' wit' a dollar and a dream in the game, you playin' wit' your *life*.

DD: One more question. It has been said by many people that Dutch isn't dead. Many believe that the police decided to cover his escape by saying he's dead because they couldn't allow people to think someone could have the kind of audacity to try something like that and get away with it. What do you think?

R: [Rahman laughs again.] People think Tupac and Elvis alive, too. People don't like to let go.

DD: But what do *you* think? Do you believe Dutch is dead?

R: [Rahman took another long pause before he answered me.] I believe many things, but to say "belief" in relation to Dutch implies hope, and as much as I loved Dutch . . . and in some ways still do, I no longer wish him on this world . . . But for their sake, they better hope he is.

CONCLUSION: FRANCE

◆

Craze held the issue of the *Don Diva* magazine in his hands. He scanned Roc's article once more, closed the magazine, and looked at Roc on the cover. It was a special edition dedicated to Dutch. The whole issue was based on Dutch. The cover read:

IS DUTCH REALLY DEAD?

Craze smiled, then closed the magazine. He was standing on the balcony of his hotel suite, looking down over the Paris night.

The balcony on which he stood had once been occupied by kings and queens, who once reigned from it. It made him think back to how it all started. They had dared to do the impossible and made it look easy. Had taken on any and all, meeting every challenge and winning them all. Now he was dining with international players and romancing women who only knew one word in English.

His name.

But he knew it wasn't over. He knew there were those who

wouldn't rest until they knew the answer to the question on the *Don Diva* cover, and knew for sure. But whatever the future held, he felt confident. Confident that no one could stop them now. They had come too far. He remembered Dutch's words from years before . . . *Ain't no turning back now.*

He heard the door of the suite open and close. He walked back into the room to greet the three surviving Charlies, accompanied by the man he had walked through hell with and emerged on the other side with, unscathed.

Dutch.

Craze handed Dutch the magazine. He looked at the picture of Roc on the cover.

"Even Roc think you dead," Craze said, as he pulled out a cigarette and checked his pockets for a light. Dutch pulled out the lighter he had taken from Mrs. Piazza. It was the same lighter he used to signal the Charlies, at the trial.

He held it up while Craze lit his cigarette from it. Craze blew out a smoke ring as Dutch replied, "They can't stop what they can't see."

Then . . . he smiled.

READING GROUP GUIDE

1. Do you think Dutch was a true thug in his heart, or just a regular guy from the hood who could have gone either way?

2. Could Dutch have established himself without brutally killing Kazami?

3. Do you think Delores could have done more to keep Dutch from the life he grew to lead?

4. Was Angel's loyalty based on true friendship or her feelings for Dutch?

5. Would you have gone to jail for life to protect someone else? If so, for who and why?

6. What do you think made Nina different from the other women Dutch dated? Why do you think she gained his heart, when even Angel could not?

7. Do you think Nina genuinely loved Dutch or loved his money and power?

8. Do you think Roberto knew who Dutch would become? That said, do you think people realize how much they influence the youth around them?

9. Why do you think the people of New Jersey went crazy when Dutch was arrested? Shouldn't the neighborhood want someone like Dutch off the streets?

10. Do you agree with Roc's decision to leave the game? Why or why not?

11. Did you find yourself rooting for Dutch in the end? If so, why?

12. Were you happy with the ending? Why or why not?

Don't miss the second book
in Teri Woods's critically acclaimed
Dutch series!

Please turn this page
for a preview of

Dutch II: Angel's Revenge

Available March 2010

PROLOGUE

Get these people out of here!" Detective Smalls bellowed.
The Essex County Courthouse had become a mad-
house. Screams of confusion and cries of pain filled the air
and seared the ears of the seasoned detective. In all of his
thirteen years on the force, he had never seen anything
like this. It was like a terrorist had dropped a bomb on the
courthouse and transformed it into a war zone. Paramedics,
uniformed police officers, and Newark's Special Unit, along
with the Newark Fire Department, all struggled to maintain order in the aftermath of the massacre.

"Move aside, please. Move aside!" Smalls commanded as
he directed the curious who had filed into the bullet-riddled
courtroom door.

"Officer! Officer! My son was in there, please . . ."

"Please don't let my wife be dead! Someone help me!"

The faces and voices reminded Smalls of a recurring
nightmare, one he could not wake up from. He had been
one of the first on the scene and had seen the human remains
strewn like discarded waste. As he entered the smoke-filled
courtroom, the smell of death hit him in the face. It now

lingered in his nostrils as he looked around in disbelief. The tragedy was an unbelievable sight.

Frank Sorbonno's body lay grotesquely twisted against the rear wall. District Attorney Anthony Jacobs's body had been blown to pieces, his headless remains sprawled on the prosecution's table. The judge was slumped over his gavel, and nine of the twelve jury members leaned every which way on top of one another.

Innocent bystanders and the disguised Charlies lay strewn on the floor. Their blood was splattered all over the courtroom and even on the American flag that hung limp in the corner. That sight in particular caught Smalls's eye and etched itself in his memory.

Smalls sat down in the back row of the courtroom and ran his hand through his salt-and-pepper hair. *How could this have happened?* he asked himself as he continued to inspect the room. Dutch had single-handedly taken the American justice system and slapped it with his bloody hand. If gunshots had been applause, the courtroom would have received a deadly standing ovation with Dutch as orchestrator.

Smalls silently watched as ambulance workers rolled corpse after corpse onto soiled gurneys and out the courtroom doors. All he could think of was Dutch. He prayed he would be found among the dead. He'd give his right arm to have Dutch in front of him, bleeding, dying, and begging to atone for the atrocity he had inflicted on the flesh of the American justice system. But Dutch was nowhere to be found. The police had sealed off the building and a ten-block radius around it. The feds had stopped airline flights and bus and train departures. But all to no avail. Dutch had managed to slip through the tight noose they had meticulously prepared for him and escaped unscathed. He mocked them all.

But more than how he did it, everyone wanted to know where he had gone.

The question was very simple.

Where was Dutch?

CHAPTER ONE

Fuck all y'all!" was Dutch's emphatic verdict on the entire courtroom, and the Charlies stood ready to impose his sentence. Bullets filled the unsuspecting courtroom. Dutch pulled out the twin forty-calibers strapped under the defense table and fired into the face of the bailiff to his right as he reached for his service revolver. The second bailiff was spun off his feet by a Charlie in the front row. People leaped and ducked but to no avail because there was nowhere to hide.

Gripping both pistols like death's sickles, ready to claim his next victim, Dutch cut the judge down with a shot to the chest. "Guilty, muthafucka! Guilty!" Dutch laughed, firing a second shot that exploded the judge's head like a melon. "Gavel that, pussy!"

Anthony Jacobs felt the muzzle at the back of his head, and before he could even pray, lead filled his thoughts.

The jury was mercilessly sprayed with a barrage of gunfire by four Charlies. All the while, Dutch searched the frenzied rows looking for Frank Sorbonno. He found him crouched under a row at the rear of the courtroom. Dutch smiled down on him.

"Frankie Bonno! It's the black Al Capone, muhfucka!" Dutch quipped as he aimed the muzzle at his bald dome. "Happy Valentine's Day, sweetheart!"

"Dutch please! I—"

Bonno's cowardly plea was silenced by six hollow-point messengers of death.

Meanwhile, courthouse officers had begun to converge on the room. Shots flew through the door, killing two Charlies, while Dutch and six other Charlies made their way to the exit and out the door.

Three more Charlies, positioned in the rear of the building, were exchanging fire with several officers, clearing the way for Dutch and his team.

"Dutch, this way, baby," one of the Charlies beckoned before her lungs filled with blood from a gunshot in the back. She fell, silenced forever, as Dutch and the others made it to the stairs.

Outside, police and ambulances had arrived.

One of the ambulances, however, arrived with two Charlies dressed as EMT workers and was conveniently parked adjacent to the rear of the courthouse.

With eyes alert to the police and all their activity, Craze cautiously emerged from behind a Dumpster and opened the back door.

To the average eye, the ambulance didn't appear out of place. The melee had panicked everyone, and no one knew what to expect next . . . Certainly not an ambulance escape.

"The basement!" Dutch ordered the remaining three Charlies with him. "Make sure my man is compensated for his assistance." He smirked, then shot out the rear door and hopped into the ambulance.

Craze looked at his longtime friend, relieved that he had made it, then screamed at the Charlie in the driver's seat, "Fuck you waitin' for, tomorrow? Drive!" She flipped on the siren and sped off. As the ambulance turned the corner, Detective Smalls and his partner, Detective Meritti, skidded up and jumped out of their car ready for war.

"Where is Dutch?" Smalls demanded, but he became distracted when Detective Meritti entered the courthouse behind him. Smalls could tell by the look on his partner's face that he was the bearer of bad news. Smalls had been dealing with the press throughout the ordeal, keeping them informed of what was going on. But he had postponed leaking any information concerning Dutch until the chief of police got back to him. And today Meritti was the chief's messenger.

"What's the world coming to, eh?" Meritti asked in his Brooklyn Italian accent. "First 9/11, now this?" He scanned the crime scene in disbelief. "This is the beginning of anarchism."

Smalls agreed. "So?" he inquired, studying Meritti's blue eyes.

Meritti sat down and lit a Winston. "I can see the headlines now. 'Gangster Kills Judge and Jury and Escapes,'" he bitterly remarked with a flourish, tapping the ashes from his cigarette. "Do you know what kind of message that would send?" Meritti continued his rant. "Every fuckin' nut with a gun and half a heart will think he can do the same thing!"

Smalls nodded. "No courtroom in America will be safe. The next thing you know, people will be shooting DAs and judges in the street!"

"And rioting in county jails to bust out the kingpins," Meritti added in a tone of disgust.

Smalls knew where Meritti was going with the conversation. "I take it the chief feels the same way?" Smalls asked, already knowing he did.

Meritti nodded, watching his partner of six years, knowing what the chief was asking of him. He knew Smalls didn't like to lie. To Meritti, Smalls had always been an annoyingly honest detective.

"If I go out there and tell those people that James is dead . . . if we cover up his escape and it gets out . . ."

"It won't get out," Meritti said, cutting him off.

"But if it does?"

"It won't."

Smalls saw the logic in the decision.

Even though Dutch had committed a heinous act, if the world thought he was dead, potential copycats would think twice because Dutch didn't survive. But to Smalls, a lie was still a lie.

However, if the truth was told, Dutch would become a legend—the gangster's hero, the outlaw who blasted his way to freedom. No, Smalls's heart decided the truth couldn't be told—yet. Not until James was firmly in his grasp. For the sake of justice everywhere, the truth had to be concealed.

Smalls rose slowly, feeling the full weight of his fifty-four years in his arthritic knees.

"Okay, let's go meet the press," he said, smiling at Meritti weakly.

Meritti took one last look at the room and wondered aloud, "But *how* did he do it? There are metal detectors on every floor, even right outside this door, and he smuggled in a fuckin' arsenal? How?"

Smalls looked at Meritti with steel in his eyes. "I don't know. But I promise you, I will find out."

With that, they left the courtroom.

A botched robbery

forces a cold-blooded killer

to devise the ultimate plan . . .

Please turn this page

for a preview of

ALIBI

Available now in hardcover

PARTY'S OVER

Hey, Lance, come here, look," whispered Jeremy, standing in an alleyway pointing to a window in what appeared to be an apartment row home on the 2500 block of Somerset Street in North Philadelphia.

"What, I don't see nothing?" whispered Lance back to him.

"The window—it's cracked. It's not shut all the way, right there. You see it?" asked Jeremy as he pointed to the window. His keen vision surpassed that of Lance, who was nearsighted and unable to see far when he wasn't wearing his glasses.

"You sure they in there?" Lance asked, trying to figure out what the next move should be as an alley cat jumped out of a tree next to him, scaring the living daylights out of him. "Nigga, I know you not laughing," he said to Jeremy, who couldn't help himself.

"You shoulda seen your face . . . Naw, for real though, I'm telling you, I followed them all day. They're in there." He shook his head, showing no signs of uncertainty in his voice. "I watched them go in there with two duffel bags. They went in and they haven't come out, neither one of them. And them duffel bags they had were chunky, real chunky. They holding a lot of money or a lot of coke. Damn, they holding."

Many different thoughts rushed around in Lance's head, the first one being how much money and how much coke their competition was holding in the house. Right now, more than ever, he needed a come up. A strong come up and he knew in his heart that this was it.

"You sure it's just the two of them in there?" Lance asked again, his heart starting to beat a little faster as the adrenaline rushed through his veins.

"Man, I'm telling you. We can take these jokers. They caught off guard. They won't even see us coming. We got one chance, Lance, just one, and this is it."

Lance needed to play the whole scene out in his head. He wanted no stone to be left unturned. There could be no mistakes, no mishaps, no fuck-ups. Jeremy might be right—this just might be his one and only chance or better yet his golden opportunity to come up. Times were hard and the only nigga in the city moving weight was Simon Shuller. Simon Shuller had been getting money for years. Everyone knew it too. Not only was he the largest drug dealer in Philadelphia, he had to be the police as well. There was no way he could run drugs, dope, and numbers year after year and not be in jail by now. But he wasn't in jail and Simon Shuller, police or not, was the man with the golden hand in the city, the big kahuna with all the money, and those two unknown suspects inside the row home on Somerset were his runners.

Truth was they could have left the door wide open, 'cause anybody crazy enough to mess with anything belonging to Simon Shuller had to be plum out of their minds.

"Man, I must be crazy listening to you," said Lance, looking at Jeremy.

"Shit, you crazy if you don't, my friend. I'm telling you, we might not ever get this chance in life again. We could sneak in, take what we came for, and sneak right back out."

Lance thought for a minute longer. *Maybe Jeremy is right, we sneak in, take what we came for, and sneak back out. How hard could that be?*

"Okay, come on, let's do the damn thing," Lance commanded, feeling nothing but heart.

"That's what I'm talking about, baby boy. Don't worry, I got this caper all figured out already. Come on, let's get the car and park it close enough to make our getaway."

Up on the fire escape, Lance looked at Jeremy, who was silently cracking the window open. He turned and waved his hand for his friend to come on. He climbed through the window and into what might once have been a bathroom. Jeremy turned again, to find Lance on the fire escape climbing through the window behind him.

"What the fuck died in this motherfucker?" whispered Lance, as a foul stench filled his nostrils.

"Shh, come on," said Jeremy as he embraced his nine-millimeter and peeked around the corner of the doorway, looking like he belonged on the force.

What the fuck do this nigga think he doing?

"Whah, why you looking at me like that?"

"Nigga, you ain't no god damn Barnaby Jones and shit. What is you doing?"

"I'm trying to make sure the coast is clear, man—let me do what I do," said Jeremy, a tad bit annoyed.

What with their whispering back and forth, neither of them heard the footsteps coming down the hallway. Not until the footsteps were right on them and the bathroom door came flying open.

"What the fuck? Y'all niggas lost?" said a tall, brown-skinned fellow, wearing a Phillies jacket and Phillies baseball cap.

At first he thought they might've been crackheads, but then he saw the shiny chrome steel and knew differently.

"Shut the fuck up, before I kill you in this motherfucker," said Jeremy, quickly maneuvering his gun and pointing it straight at his victim's head. "Come on, let's go."

Jeremy held the man on his left side, close to his body. He held his gun in his right hand up to the man's head as they began walking back down the hallway. They heard another guy call out from the living room.

"Yo, Ponch, we need more vials. You gonna have to run down to the—"

His sentence was cut short as he saw his man, Poncho, being led by Jeremy and Lance through the doorway with a gun pointed at his head.

"Don't even think about it, Shorty," said Lance, pointing his gun at the guy sitting at the table stuffing tiny vials with two hits of crack.

"What the fuck?"

"Nigga, you know what it is. Bag that shit up, put it back in the duffel bag and don't nobody got to get hurt."

The man at the table, Nard, quickly surveyed everything that was going on. *These dudes ain't wearing no masks. That can only mean one thing.* And even though Jeremy and Lance's intention wasn't to kill, just rob, Nard felt otherwise and being a true thoroughbred for Simon Shuller, he'd rather die fighting than give them niggas a dime, even if the coke wasn't his. Some things in life were just more important, and his reputation for being a "real nigga" was one of them. Nard was a youngster with mad heart, and for the dough, he had love. For the streets, he had respect, and for a principle about some bullshit, he would fight tooth and nail. He slithered his arm, without a glance, under the table. Right where he had put it earlier was a tiny .22, a piece of duct tape keeping it suspended upside down. *Mmm hmm, we gonna see now, motherfucker.* Nice and smooth and just enough to do damage, he was ready, ready to pop off. Quickly, his fingers fondled the cold steel, until his grasp was tight. Nard came from under the table so fast, no one saw it coming, not even Poncho. He shot Lance one time in the chest, the bullet piercing his heart. Lance dropped to the floor holding his chest with one hand and his gun in the other, the bullet moving inside him. He looked up at Jeremy, gasping for breath and collapsing in a red pool of blood.

"Let him go, motherfucker!" shouted Nard.

"Nard, take this, nigga. Take him. I know you can, baby boy, take him," Poncho yelled.

"Shut up, shut the fuck up," said Jeremy, now nervous, as his man was gasping for air, gurgling blood, and reaching for him to help him.

"Let him go, let him go. Let him go and I'll let you live," said Nard, meaning every word he spoke, but trying to be calm as he talked Jeremy into letting his man go.

"Nigga, give me what the fuck I came for or both you

motherfuckers is gonna die," said Jeremy, with lots of heart, pushing the gun harder into the side of Poncho's head. He looked down on the floor. Lance was dead. *Oh, my god, he killed him, he killed Lance.*

"Motherfucker, I ain't giving you shit. Let him go!" Nard yelled again.

"Take him, Nard, what the fuck is you waiting fo—"

The shot from Jeremy's gun seemed unreal at first, a mistake, a misfortune, something that wasn't suppose to be, a gap, a space, time that needed to rewind. In slow motion, so slow, Jeremy felt Poncho's body slump to the floor as Nard watched Poncho, his main man, die right in front of him. Poncho's blood, and fragments of his head, landed all over the wall and covered the entire side of the room. His blood even splattered on Nard, all this within a matter of seconds.

Instinct moved through Nard, like a thief in the night, and like lightning, the bullet from that tiny .22 pierced through Jeremy's chest and threw him back several steps, as his body began to slump against the door. His fingers unable to grasp, he dropped his gun and looked down at the blood pouring out of his body, then fell to the floor, lying on his back. He stared up at the ceiling as his body stopped breathing. Jeremy didn't even see it coming, it just happened so fast. Nard hit him with the strike of magic and poof, just like that, Jeremy was gone.

"Fuck!" yelled Nard, holding his head in his right hand, his gun still in his left. "Fuck, god damn it. Fuck you come here for, stupid-ass motherfuckers?" he yelled, angrily interrogating a dead Jeremy and a dead Lance. "Damn, what the fuck am I gonna do now?"

He surveyed the room as he talked and cursed the dead

bodies around him. "Motherfuckers!" he said as he kicked a lifeless Jeremy. *What am I going to do? What the fuck?* He checked the three bodies lying on the floor for a pulse, starting with his man, Poncho.

"Damn, Ponch, man. I'm so sorry, man. I'm so sorry," he said as he felt Poncho's wrist. "I love you, man. I love you. Fuck!" He started thinking about the consequences of what had just happened. "Fucking police, man. Fuck, what am I going to do?"

He just couldn't think straight, his brain was overwhelmed, to say the least. He threw all the crack, vials, and other paraphernalia into a duffel bag that was lying under the table and left the other one, which was empty lying on the floor. He looked around the room, grabbed everything that belonged to him, tried to wipe off the table, doorknobs, and everything else he had touched in the crack spot and quickly ran out the door and down a flight of stairs.

"Hey, Nard, be careful, they shooting in the building."

He quickly turned around, his gun still in his hand, but tucked inside the front pocket of his hoodie.

"Hey, Shorty," he said as he looked at a kid standing in the vestibule. He couldn't have been more than nine, maybe ten years old. He didn't know the kid's name, but this kid knew his. "Yeah, you be careful too, kid."

He quickly brushed past him, threw his hoodie over his head, made his way out the door, and quickly walked down the street to his car.

"DaShawn, get in here! Don't you hear them shooting? Come on, boy!"

Nard looked up and saw a young black girl hanging out

a window, hollering for the same young kid that Nard had just brushed past inside the building.

"I'm coming, Ma. I'm right here."

Nard could hear the little boy as he walked away from the spot.

Please tell me this kid ain't no problem, or the window chick. Fuck, man, fuck! I need me an alibi. And where the fuck is Sticks? Simon is gonna be heated, but at least I got his coke. That's all I need to do is get at Simon. I got to get rid of this gun, too. Yeah, that's all I'll need is an alibi and I'm good.

ABOUT THE AUTHOR

While working as a legal secretary for a law firm and juggling motherhood in Philadelphia, PA, Teri Woods completed her first novel, *True to the Game*. Teri submitted her story over a period of six years to more than twenty different publishers, all of whom rejected it. In 1998, Teri printed, bound, self-published, and began selling her book from the trunk of her car on the streets of Philadelphia and New York.

With support and encouragement of friends, Teri started her own publishing company, Meow Meow Productions, which later became Teri Woods Publishing. In the fall of 2007, Teri joined Grand Central Publishing, formerly known as Warner Books, with the re-release of *True to the Game*, as well as *True to the Game II*, *True to the Game III*, and Teri's first hardcover, *Alibi*.

As the owner of Teri Woods Publishing, Teri has published twelve novels: *True to the Game*, *Dutch*, *Dutch II*, *Deadly Reigns I*, *Deadly Reigns II*, *Angel*, *B-More Careful*, *The Adventures of Ghetto Sam*, *Triangle of Sins*, *Rectangle of Sins*, *Tell Me Your Name*, and *Double Dose*. *True to the Game*, *B-More Careful*, *Dutch*, *Triangle of Sins*, *Rectangle of Sins*, *Deadly*

Reigns I, Deadly Reigns II, and *Angel* have been featured on the *Essence* bestseller list numerous times collectively. *True to the Game II* and *True to the Game III* both hit the *New York Times* bestseller list.

Teri currently resides in New Jersey with her three children and is hard at work on her next novel.